<0 C0 AKT 338

Semitones

Derek Furr

Art
Andrés San Millán

Fomite

Burlington, Vermont

Copyright 2015 by © Derek Furr

All rights reserved. No part of this book may be reproduced in any form or by any means without the prior written consent of the publisher, except in the case of brief quotations used in reviews and certain other non-commercial uses permitted by copyright law.

ISBN-13: 978-1-942515-03-6
Library of Congress Number : 2015947754

Fomite
58 Peru Street
Burlington, VT 05401
www.fomitepress.com

Cover and interior art – Andrés San Millán

The author gratefully acknowledges the following magazines and journals, where some of this work was previously published: *Anthem, The Broome Review, Cider Press Review, Diagram, Field Notes, Roanoke Review* and *The Vision.*

"Now the usual Intervals are in number 9, viz. a Semitone, and that is a rising from one Voyce to another (by an imperfect second) sounding flatly: and it is only betwixt the Voyces Mi, fa. It is called a Semitone, not because it is half a Tone, (for a Tone cannot be divided into two equal parts), but because it is an imperfect Tone..."

— John Dowland (1609)

Contents

Cassandra

Every day, in all seasons, a woman paces the sidewalks uptown. She moves quickly, staring ahead, looking distressed, as though there is something to be reported. Every half-block, always where two sections of bluestone meet, she stops abruptly and presses her palms into the small of her back. Like the farmer's wife behind the plow, she turns her gaze upwards, gaunt, wide-eyed, skin baked and chafed, Dorothea Lange's migrant mother. She comes down again, watches a few cars pass—perhaps she counts—then resumes her look of distress, her pacing.

She is usually silent, but once I heard a terrible keening and knew it was she. She passed beneath my window during a snowstorm, having deviated from her customary route. She gripped her head and covered her ears to shut out the voice of one I couldn't hear, one who had drawn close enough to her not to be ignored. She sped up, slowed down, turned, gesticulated furiously, wailed and ululated, a Banshee, warning us.

What blew along in front of her, spiraling upward in

chromatic divagations? Ghost figures, papery wind riders, Chagall's levitating couples. They catch in bare branches and gather in corners we rarely clean. Some say they are angels, some the dead, some need more evidence to call them anything at all. She shrieks toward my window, "You say you cannot see them? Your eyes are fevered. Rub them with new fallen snow." Or so I imagine.

When I was a child, fever woke me at midnight with an aspect of the devil. I reached for my cap gun. I was shivering like one possessed, and could do nothing about it but call to my father for help. "Mein Vater, Mein Vater, und hoerst du nicht?" Addled and earnest, he rushed in, assessed the situation, and sat by me. When I woke up again, he was still there, having stayed until daybreak brought one more tale of childhood fears to an end.

I didn't respond to her. By the time I gathered the nerve, she had wandered off. Who is to say what we fail to see, what we do not hear, hesitant and silent behind our windows? "We are closed in," writes Yeats, "and the key is turned/On our uncertainty…" On the other side are many voices, a chorus of semitones. What key are they seeking?

Dawn Chorus

Aubade

Leaves like lashes fluttered around the robin, grey-breasted
before sunrise, an eye for the maple, also grey, to observe
with me a spider securing the lasts of its web to hosta stalks
against the breeze.

Then came the mechanical elephant in a waistcoat
walking erect, drumming, in the attitude of one
reciting multiplication tables at the end of third grade.

"Okay, I shall suffer courageously," pledged the damselfly
caught in the orb, glad of an audience and rhythm.

The robin dove at the elephant. The spider descended.
Blind, the maple greened.

The Annunciation to Mary of Upstate New York (as she prepared her essay for ART 554 Women in Renaissance Religious Painting)

Appearing at first as a wren, the angel in a noiseless trans-mutation reached its full size and form as it entered my room from its perch on the windowsill. Just as the Old Masters have shown, it had wings and a halo, but otherwise its features were human and androgynous, its delicacy and unblemished skin conventionally feminine, its stature and assertiveness masculine. Its wings, rooted at the scapulae, classed it with the Gabriels of Fra Lippo Lippi and Fra Giovanni Angelico, in whose Annunciations the feathers are brightly colored. Extending the full length of its body, the wings remained always extruded, even when the angel was at rest, awaiting my response to its message.

Remarking the unsurpassed beauty of Fra Giovanni's figures, Vasari argues that in painting the sanctified, one is obligated to show a per-fection far beyond that of the fallen world. He parts ways with those who, "seeing figures of women or youths adorned with loveliness or beauty beyond the ordinary, straight-way censure them and judge them licentious," although he does allow that nudity has no place in church paintings, "even although a man has to show how much he knows."

That is not at all how it happened, although the angel was initially a wren and the wings did resemble Gabriel's from the San Marco Annunciation of Angelico. The casement shattered during the transmutation and drove a splinter the size of a pencil into the angel's right hip. There was no blood but the screech, while surely justified, was nonetheless infernal, not what one might expect from a being sent, presumably, from above. Without forethought, I grabbed the splinter and pulled it out, sending a spray of electric sparks across the room that singed the rug in several spots. Apologetic and grateful, the angel touched lightly down, and as we discussed its message, the burns repaired themselves in its aura.

While William Michael Rossetti has nothing to say about a saint's state of undress or an artist's pretensions to forbidden knowledge, he would have preferred to find a blemish or a look of mild consternation among the elect in Angelico's paintings. Noting that Angelico's art is pietistic, Rossetti writes in his 1911 Britannica entry on the painter, "His visages have an air of rapt suavity, devotional fervency and beaming esoteric consciousness, which is intensely attractive to some minds and realizes beyond rivalry a particular ideal—that of ecclesiastical saintliness and detachment from secular fret and turmoil."

There was no transmutation. The wren, <u>Thryothorus</u> <u>ludovicianus</u>, was a juvenile female. Her halo, which resembled a wedding band, clinked the windowpane. I declared myself a skeptic. Against the glass the wren pressed the underside of her wing, which was lined with iridescent feathers that refracted the lamplight. I opened the window. It was cold. The wren fluttered in and lit on the frayed spine of a dictionary, the floor being crowded with leaning towers of books. From her beak dangled a pink thread, woolen, as if unraveled from a winter mitten.

Angelico's Mary, in his many treatments of the Annunciation, stands outside both of these descriptions, having neither a figure of celestial beauty nor a face that beams "esoteric consciousness." Shoulders narrow and rounded, hands loosely crossed in front of her abdomen, she gazes at the messenger with quiet concern. She is pensive and plain, that is her beauty. She will not break into song. There is in the deep background at her eye level a small window beyond an open doorway. It looks onto a dark forest. She does not turn to it, but it centers our gaze as the eye of the angel centers hers. I have concentrated on that window, and I have begun to see its purpose and what lies beyond it.

The wren, God's messenger, came through the window and

placed the thread in my palm. She sang these words to me, "Your heart is a nest, a gathering of this and that into perfect form, in which the slightest pink thread, snatched by a mother from her child's unraveling mitten and dropped in the slush, contributes tensity, warmth, even extravagance. The color of this nest, the weave of aluminum foil and broomstraw, none of this is incidental. Within is a wren, watchful, but its eyes glint with the curiosity of the unafraid, settled as in the palm of a hand, free to fly or be quietly enclosed. Her curved beak can spear the spider, a delicacy. And as an emblem of the heart's chambers, in the nest there are four eggs, smooth and densely freckled as the cheeks of a redhead, secret and hopeful. Without melancholy she broods, for she has made all this."

So I came to understand why I had been studying these paintings, why I loved Angelico's Mary, her serious eyes, her hands like my hands, *folded as sea waves that gather*
to a place of overlap, or as the tips of a wren's wings that cross when she rests, and I set aside my papers and my books, *for my hands O Lord are yours to increase, to speed,*
to warm, to put to use.

Become a Light

1

Sean snapped his briefcase as he stood in the doorway of the bedroom. He had raised the blind, and the sunlight filtering through the hydrangea made shadow puppets on Alanis' bedsheet. Her body was tiny and crumpled beneath it. The black mass of her hair washed up on her pillow and covered her face.

"I have to go give the final exam, Alanis. I'll come home as soon as it's over. I love you. We can figure this out."

Was she asleep? Threads of black floated and descended. So she was breathing. Ghostly animals scurried along her motionless form.

Alanis had stopped getting out of bed, and Sean didn't know what else to do. He had already taken two sick days this week to keep watch on her. She wouldn't eat or drink. She wouldn't respond to anything he said. Even now, when he squeezed her foot gently as a gesture of farewell, she just lay there facing the wall. He pulled the door closed behind him.

Sean did not know that Alanis had miscarried. He had not, in fact, known that she was pregnant. She had not been far along, but she had grown hopeful and intended to keep the baby despite the fact that Sean was not the father. Algie Williams was.

Algie had seduced her at their 20-year high school reunion. Or rather, Alanis had led him to believe she was seduced. It made him incautious, which is what she needed. She knew he would disappear back to the west coast the next morning and not rear his manhood near her again for at least a decade. Under the influence of five bourbon and gingers, she had been liberated into this solution to her and Sean's childlessness. Although the odds were obviously against her, Algie was nothing if not virile. She had gambled that his sperm would strike the bullseye if anyone's could.

She and Algie had not dated each other in high school, just pursued ways of having sex furtively while going steady with Sean and Beata. No one knew, so no one suffered. Sean and Algie were drafted shortly after graduation. Algie broke up with Beata, and Sean and Alanis got engaged. When Sean returned from Vietnam, Alanis had become pregnant right away with Lily. It was to be the start of a big family. They had bought the green-trimmed Cape Cod near St. Joseph's, the high school where Sean got a position teaching history. Five bedrooms were more than they could afford on Sean's salary at the time, but Alanis' parents made up the difference. During Alanis' pregnancy, as an infant, as a toddler, Lily had been sweet and easy. She had thick, jet-black hair, enough for a ribbon by the time she was twenty months old and Alanis was pregnant again.

Then, over Thanksgiving, 1977, Sean brought home the flu. It killed Lily and caused Alanis' first miscarriage. Alanis tried not to blame Sean, and Sean tried to reason himself out of accepting blame. But the presumption of guilt settled on him. Intimacy, in its fumbling and desperate returns, brought no more children. In the beginning, it hadn't mattered. To Alanis, the idea of new children was an offense against those she had lost. How dare she love another? And for that matter, the risk of more loss was so present to her that she could hear it scratching at the windowpane when she and Sean made love. Sorrow and fear were slow to abate. Now, nearly fifteen years after Lily's death, Alanis felt a fool for her new ache. Hadn't they been fortunate in other ways? The house was paid for. Her real estate business was steady and occupied much of her time. Sean was chair of the history department at St. Joseph's. She and Sean had formed a sad but loving friendship that could sustain them into old age. The fact is that a scrim of disappointment shaded even the brightest couples among their friends. Alanis concluded that at least Sean's and her dimness had a source one could point to.

But the ache. A baby, one she could claim to be theirs, would assuage it. She and Sean could begin again, however belatedly, without rehearsing their regrets and lacing their bed with yet more anxiety. She hadn't seen or even talked to Algie before the night of the reunion. The plan came to her in the moment. Then it was fuck and flee, just as in high school, except she had hoped to get pregnant rather than prayed not to. She took no pleasure in Algie this time, and neither was there any shame, even after she sobered up. This was about recovery from the losses she and Sean had endured. As soon as the test came back positive, Alanis had slept with Sean, almost jubilantly. She let him come to her, night after night, and his surprise at her passion might have offended her except that she could feel the baby becoming theirs.

Now there was a third among the tiny ghosts that flitted in and out of her dreams. The ghosts of her babies were faceless, even Lily, whose features had wasted away despite Alanis' pledge to meditate daily on her photograph. Often the ghosts had no bodies, no visible form, but she could hear them, their pulse and desperation to return to her. They raced inside her like breath on a frigid morning and lingered in that way. They whimpered inconsolably. She was trying now to quiet them, lying as still as she could, turning her back to the light from the bedroom window and thinking, *Hush little babies don't say a word, Mama's going to buy you a mockingbird.* She could hear Sean speaking to her from the doorway, but she could not make out his meaning. The whimpers swelled at the sound of his voice. Poor Sean. He hadn't known. He hadn't meant to. But hadn't it been his heat, his thrusts, just as it had been his flu the first time around? He was a carrier, innocent but deadly.

2

When Sean returned, later than he'd hoped, there was a Sprite can next to the bed and an empty ring in the six pack in the refrigerator. Alanis must have been up today while he gave the exam. He closed the bedroom door again and stood gazing down the hall. Dust motes drifted in shafts of sunlight like tiny parachutists. They disappeared into shadows before he could see them land. Under the window was a small statue of the Buddha. It stood among bills, loose change, and other pocket discharge on the letter stand. It had come to Sean in Vietnam.

His platoon was scouring a village, rounding up Vietcong. The order was to take men and older boys into custody long enough to have them interrogated by two South Vietnamese soldiers assigned to their mission. The soldiers fanned out, three per tiny thatched hut, Sean the leader of his small squadron. Several houses into the search, all the squadrons had turned up only small children, mothers, and the elderly, noisy chickens and underfed milk goats. It was a village without men. Where had they gone? The first woman's answer to that question was echoed by everyone subsequently: all the men disappeared with the last raid by American G.I. Joe imperialists. It wasn't a satisfactory response, because intelligence said otherwise. The village was believed to be a supply hub. There was no record of a former raid by U.S. soldiers.

Orders were to use deadly force only in self-defense. But by the time Sean and his two buddies entered their ninth hut, fear and frustration were getting the better of the platoon. Someone in the trio across the muddy road fired a few rounds into the air. There was a scream, followed by wailing. Sean counted the people in his house: a mother, a baby, an aged woman hunched on a mat, and a teenage boy. That boy was the first male over ten years old they'd seen in the village, and with all the commotion as forewarning, he nonetheless lay there in plain view. Sean's men had their rifles trained on him. He was lying on his side on a cot, bareback and bare legged, covered with small cuts and bruises. His face was swollen. He stared through Sean. His hands were beneath the pillow under his head.

Again machine guns rattled angrily outside, and a child shrieked. "Show your hands, kid!" It was Jackson. His voice shook. He motioned repeatedly with his rifle barrel. The boy continued to stare. "Show your fucking hands!"

"Jack, you dumbass, he doesn't understand," Sean called back. "Just keep your rifle on him. Friedman, go get the translators."

Sean walked over to the cot. The boy tensed up, but his eyes were motionless. The old woman was now calmly reciting, over and over, a phrase Sean soon figured out though he spoke no Vietnamese. The boy was blind. But he could hear the commotion. Why not at least sit up? Sean shoved his hands under the pillow. The boy's fists were clinched and his pulse thumped wildly. Still he said nothing. The screams and gunfire outside were amplified by their hearts racing as Sean yanked so hard that the boy flipped off the cot like a fish and lay gasping for air. In his hands was the statue, a sandalwood Buddha.

The old woman shouted something new, and the boy dropped the statue at Sean's feet. Jackson shot the boy through the head before realizing that the Buddha was not a grenade.

Two decades later, the sunlight haloed the Buddha, a decoration on Sean's letter stand.

Sean glared at the bedroom door. What had Alanis endured that he had not, and more? If anyone had a reason not to get up, it was he. He wanted to say that to Alanis. No, he didn't want to say it so much as he felt that she should simply realize it. All that love-making, so unusual for them in the years since they lost the children—he had concluded that it was Alanis' way of trying again for a baby. Why wouldn't she just say that? Probably she didn't want to hear him caution her against hope. He couldn't blame her for that. But the outcome was predictable, and he couldn't bear a resurgence of her depression, so many years after Lily's death and the miscarriage. Why was he the one who had simply to endure? He wanted to say to her, "You get up. That's what you do—you just keep getting up. There's nothing for it but that." Of course if she looked to his example, surely she could see there was no other way forward. You took responsibility and tried not to hurt anyone twice. You accepted what you couldn't control.

3

When the doorbell rang the tenth time, Alanis crawled out of bed. She couldn't ignore it, much as she tried, any more than she could disappear into the heavy air of the bedroom.

She assumed that Sean was locked out, but at the door was a teenage girl dressed completely in black: black Converse sneakers, jeans, and t-shirt, ebony nails, eyeliner and lipstick. The single exception was a sparkling orange barrette that pulled her long black hair back from her forehead. She was pregnant.

"I need to see Mr. Kilpatrick," she said.

"You're one of his students?"

"Yes."

"Shouldn't you check at school?"

The girl raised an eyebrow. "So he goes into school on Saturday mornings?"

Alanis blushed. "I forgot it was Saturday." His car was missing from the driveway. "Maybe he stepped out to buy the paper. How did you find us?"

"This is a bad time. I'll come back later."

"No. I'm sorry for being so addled. I've been sick. Why don't you come in and wait a few minutes?"

The girl rubbed her belly unconsciously. "You could give him a message. You can say, 'Suzanne came to see you.' He'll understand."

"Really? Was he expecting you? If it's important, I'm sure he would want you to stay and tell him yourself."

Suzanne shook her head. "Just give him the message, please. He'll understand it. I've gotten you up, and you don't look well. No offense. You should go back to bed."

How she must appear! Ashen and disheveled, pajamas wrinkled from days of continuous wear, her eyes sunken and dark. She had to prop herself against the doorpost, her body was so weak from hunger. She smelled unwashed.

Only now, her mind braced by this pregnant student asking after her husband, did Alanis remember hearing about

Suzanne from Sean—not that she was pregnant, but that she was one of his better students and she had gone AWOL. Several weeks ago, Sean had accompanied the social worker to Suzanne's house, a small, dilapidated bungalow near the old textile mill. The porch was stacked with cast off furniture and appliances. One of the couches served as a collection space for empty Wild Turkey bottles. Through the screen door, they could see the aunt, asleep in a lawn chair in front of the television. The TV volume and the roar of a window fan drowned out their rapping at the door. The social worker took a nail file from her purse and wedged it in to dislodge the hook from the eye and gain them entrance—illegally, Sean assumed, but the door did pop open, and after all, who would really care? She turned down *Jeopardy!* and woke the aunt.

"Ain't seen her in a month," the aunt declared, after waking enough to roll a cigarette and offer her guests instant coffee, which they politely refused. "I figure she's run off with some boy. She's old enough to get her self into trouble and out of it, I figure."

The social worker began to speak about the legal obligations of a guardian, but the aunt cut her off.

"Miss, I ain't no more that rag doll's guardian than I'm yourn. It's just her bad luck or mine, depending on how you look at it, that I'm her only kin folk. Besides, Suzanne's 18. She can come and go as she pleases."

Sean spoke of how bright Suzanne was, how she showed such promise for college. The aunt was unmoved. Pouring whiskey into a pink plastic cup, she replied, "Promise ain't never kept anyone from making bad decisions, especially if the bad decision is what you really want. If my niece shows up again, I'll let her know ya'll stopped. But until then, I've helped you as much as I'm able." She turned up the TV volume.

Alanis recalled the story as Suzanne walked down the driveway, and Sean pulled in. The glare of the mid-morning sun off his windshield momentarily blinded Alanis, and as her eyes slowly recovered, her husband and the pregnant girl were grainy shades suspended in brightness. Sean was dedicated to his students, especially the difficult ones, and his anger and disappointment when they failed were measures of his heavy investment in their welfare. But when had he made a home visit to any other student? When had any other student ever shown up at their house on a Saturday?

A pregnant girl at that, one who spoke cryptically. "He'll understand."

Alanis had her secrets. Maybe he had his.

In the long conversation that followed in the living room, Suzanne would not discuss her extended absence from school except to say that she had "been on a journey to sort things out." She had returned to find that her aunt was gone and the house was now occupied by crackheads.

Mr. Kilpatrick had been kind to her at school, and she just needed a place to stay for a few days while she applied for public assistance.

Sean sat stony-faced until Suzanne finished her narrative. He then brought up the father. Not that it was any of their business, he said, but since she was asking such a favor of him and Alanis, he felt he needed to find out. Was the father not in a position to pitch in, at least financially? Sean and Alanis could go with Suzanne to talk to him if their support would make it easier for her.

Suzanne shook her head. "The baby's father cannot help in those ways. He won't."

Alanis looked at Sean, whose brow was furrowed in what she called his teacher stare. "I'm not following you. He can't or he won't?"

"I mean that this is mine to sort out. I just need a place to stay. It should only be a couple of days."

Sean persisted, "Do you mean that the father is refusing to help? Or did this happen without your consent?"

For the first time since she arrived, the girl seemed to lose her composure. She glanced over at Alanis, who felt an urge to protect her. "Sean, no, that's not yours to ask. Suzanne, you don't have to answer that."

Suzanne shook her head again. Her hands trembled, and the look in her eye now seemed to plea for understanding.

"I told you I left town to sort things out. It was a mission, really. A journey. I can't say more about it except that the child I'm carrying is special. I've been chosen to bring her into the world."

Sean frowned. " 'Chosen'? Suzanne, I know you're a Catholic school girl, and this is serious business, but let's not make it more than it is. You have to level with us if you want our help."

"Sean, don't be officious," Alanis asserted. "I think it's fine to give her a day or two to rest up. We don't have to know everything, certainly not yet, and not if she doesn't want us to know."

Suzanne studied Sean and Alanis' faces. "I'm not being dishonest. It's just complicated, and I need a place to stay for a few days. Nothing more than that."

Sean leaned forward. "It will turn into more than that. These things always do. So if you're in trouble, or the father is, you have to trust us enough to tell us."

"It's not like that, Mr. Kilpatrick. You have to trust me. Just a few days…"

"…which will become a few weeks. Unless this is an immaculate conception, and you're carrying the second coming, I'm not inclined to be the innkeeper until we get social services and whatever's left of your family involved. Do you have any idea where your aunt is?"

"Sean, stop!" Alanis shouted. "What has gotten into you? Why are you trying so hard not to help her? Didn't you make a house call on Suzanne not long ago?"

Suzanne blushed. "You came to my aunt's house?"

Alanis leaned into Sean. "She clearly still needs help. Maybe more than that social worker knew. Maybe more than you knew. She's only asking for a couple of days."

Sean was momentarily speechless. Alanis moved next to Suzanne. She gazed down at the bulge and back at Sean. "Honey, you can stay in our spare bedroom. It was our daughter's. I'll need to move a few things. You can stay there until we can find you a better situation."

Sean bristled. "Now wait just a goddamn minute, Alanis. You're in no state to make rational decisions. You've lain in bed, brooding, for days. Don't think I don't know why." He paused and stood up, as if to emphasize his point, then sat down again. "Suzanne, it's not like I haven't already tried to help you. You're bright, you're on the road to acing my course, then you disappear for weeks, miss the final, and turn up pregnant at my door on a Saturday morning. I've taught plenty of teenagers in my time, and I can turn your situation into a plausible story. Mine does not involve missions and holy spirits descending like a dove. Alanis says we're willing to help, and I know the way to do it. There's a women's shelter in Rocky Mount. I'll drive you there."

Suzanne got up to leave. "Don't bother, Mr. Kilpatrick. If I thought that was right, I would do it on my own."

"Don't get indignant. You've asked us to help, and we're offering it."

"Sean, there's no 'us' in your reaction."

"Mr. Kilpatrick, I thought you were compassionate enough to spare a room for a few days. That's all."

Alanis took Suzanne's hand and pulled her back from the door. "I said you could stay, and you'll stay." Her eyes were on Sean as she spoke. "Mr. Kilpatrick and I have some things to discuss. I have been sick, and Mr. Kilpatrick and I have been a little out of touch because of it. But you should stay. It will give a purpose to my days to fix up that room again, especially for a girl in need. I insist."

Sean moved aside as Alanis led Suzanne down the hall. He slammed the door when he left.

4

Sean was the father. Alanis saw it clearly. For the rest of the day and into the night, she replayed the living room scene from every angle, at a distance and up close. And the version that astonished her, the one that outshone even her own scheme with Algie, had Sean improvising a way to shelter Suzanne and care for his child in exchange for her promise of secrecy. He had wanted exactly what Alanis ended up offering. His condescending treatment of Suzanne, his overwrought language, it was all a performance, masterfully bad, so much so that by the end Alanis wanted to play along even as she grew increasingly suspicious of his behavior. She actually wanted poor Suzanne to stay.

It was first-rate theatre, realistic, believable, except that no version of Sean she had ever known would have slept with his student. Never. She knew that Sean had despaired of their tepid romantic life. His unbounded glee in their recent brief resurgence was energized by years of repression. But even if he had been tempted by Suzanne, an "if" she could barely credit, he would not take such unfair advantage. He wouldn't stoop to that, not the Sean she had befriended and loved for nearly two decades. Her clarity about his character was enough to undermine her faith in what she had witnessed.

So when Sean came back, she did not confront him. She would wait to see how things unfolded. He would likely do the same. It was a familiar pattern in their disagreements. And as for Suzanne, he would say nothing to her now. He would consider her to be Alanis' charge.

Toward Suzanne, Alanis felt no animosity or jealousy. Whatever the narrative—Sean was the father, a teenage boy or forgotten abusive uncle was the father, God was the father— the girl was faultless. She was worldly beyond her years and in over her head. As their lodger, Suzanne kept to herself. She ate very little and, after the first evening, always on her own. She politely turned down offers to join her hosts at dinner or by the TV. She would not accept rides to the doctor or the DSS. She walked or took the bus and brought back her own modest stock of groceries. She rarely left Lily's room, and despite the hours she spent there, she only altered one thing about it: she pulled the rocking chair over to the window.

The view was limited. There was a propane tank, striped black and white, and a clothesline that served exclusively as a perch for starlings. Beyond this was a large meadow that separated Sean and Alanis' house from the back yards of other houses in the neighborhood. Deer frequented it in the early morning and fed on the brambles. Suzanne rocked for hours every day in front of the window, her Walkman on.

Alanis understood the rocking and the stare, and after a week of passing by the door, knocked on it loudly enough to get Suzanne's attention.

"I'm afraid there's not much to see out that window."

"No. But I'm actually kind of glad of that."

"Oh?"

"Mrs. Kilpatrick, is there something you wanted?"

"No, no. I'm just concerned that you spend so much of every day at that window. Please feel free to sit in the living room or watch TV. You have a spare key. It's fine to go out, meet up with friends."

"It's getting harder to walk. I'm fine with sitting here."

"Just don't let loneliness get to you. I'm sorry I can't be better company. I got behind during my illness. I have another client to meet today."

"DSS says that an apartment will be vacant in Rose House in two weeks. It's longer than I had intended to impose on you, but it's all there is locally."

"Suzanne, you are not imposing."

"Mr. Kilpatrick thinks differently."

"No, honey. No he doesn't. He feels responsible."

Suzanne flipped the cassette in her Walkman. "I don't know why he would. Or why you would. I'll be provided for."

"Mr. Kilpatrick and I have been together for 20 years. We've endured a lot. Especially where children are concerned. Has he said a single word about you leaving since that first day? Not to me. He would have you stay."

"No offense, Mrs. Kilpatrick, but even if I believed that, I would move to Rose House when the room is ready."

"It's a nice enough facility. But you could stay here."

"I need to be independent with this. It's my mission. I have to fulfill it on my own."

"Suzanne, let's be honest. I think you came here because you wanted Mr. Kilpatrick's help. I mean his help, specifically."

As on the day she arrived, Suzanne seemed to study Alanis' face. Alanis felt it and didn't look away. "Mrs.

Kilpatrick, you wonder why I sit by this window. It's something about this room. I sensed it the moment I set down my backpack. I haven't asked you what happened to Lily. But in the only picture of her in here, she's a toddler. Did she die?"

Alanis turned to the picture. It was a Christmas photo. Lily wore a green felt dress and white stockings. Her hair was in pigtails tied with red ribbon. She stood next to the tree and held one of the ornaments. Alanis became suddenly hollow and cold. All she could remember of that day, of that moment, was in the photo. Nothing more remained.

"Her spirit is in here, Mrs. Kilpatrick. Her energy. When I'm rocking by this window, I am as aware of it as I am of you right now."

Alanis blanched. She grabbed the arm of the rocking chair. "Do not say such things to me, Suzanne. Maybe you mean well. But don't say such things."

Suzanne did seem surprised. "I didn't mean any harm, Mrs. Kilpatrick."

Alanis let go of the rocker. "I know. These things are hard. You came for Mr. Kilpatrick's help. But I'm your advocate, Suzanne. I don't need any more of your story to be convinced that letting you stay here is the right thing. But I can't share any more either."

Suzanne nodded. "I'm fine sitting here by the window, Mrs. Kilpatrick." She put on her headphones and pressed play.

A tinny thumping and buzz seemed to signal to Alanis to go.

She backed out of the bedroom and wandered down the hall. She began tidying the cluttered letter stand. The bills had gone unpaid. She would have to do something about that soon.

She picked up the Buddha and dusted him with the hem of her blouse. His eyes were closed. She had never noticed. She brushed them with her fingers. Sean had told her the story of his Buddha on the night Lily died. It was the only battle tale he had ever told her. They were standing right here, in the dark, after watching Lily's body be taken from the hospital room to the coroner. They had dripped the faucet so the pipes wouldn't freeze, and that was the only sound in the house before he started talking. It was as if he were off at a distance—she distinctly remembered that sensation. A disembodied voice, telling her about a platoon's loss of discipline, explaining in minute detail the way the blind boy's head shattered and sprayed blood and bone fragments all over his family. He and Jackson had left them wailing, coddling the body, and stumbled absently to the next hut and the next to continue their searching. At the end of the mission, he realized he had the Buddha in his hand. He had held it the whole time. He had no idea where his rifle was.

He had told her this and walked off to their bedroom by himself.

Now she felt that she understood why he told her the story in that moment, and she hated it. She hated what he was willing to accept. They were the parents of dead children. It was what they had to bear as a consequence of going on. Maybe she had believed that, tacitly, for twenty years. But in Lily's room today there was a different possibility, another future. Maybe he had provided it. Regardless, she chose to take it.

5

Sean was up at 4:30 making coffee. Going back to sleep seemed unlikely. Witnessing the various hours of the night, the look of the sky and neighborhood...he had to glean some sort of benefit from insomnia. This took him to the back door, which stood open, although he was certain he had closed and locked it before bed. He stepped out onto the porch. An hour yet until sunrise, but the dawn chorus had already started. The moon was full and glowed on the hundreds of spider webs woven into the damp meadow grasses. There was a small herd of deer, and in the midst of them stood Suzanne.

Sean stepped off the porch and into the meadow. The damp grass soaked his pajama legs. A flock of field sparrows burst up from the ground in front of him. In one motion, all the deer looked at him and leapt away, leaving Suzanne staring at him.

"How do you get them to come up to you like that? Are you feeding them?"

"No. I come into the meadow and they come up to me. It's not the first time."

Sean gazed around the meadow. The deer were scattered along the perimeter, all of them cautiously watching him.

"Are you out here every morning?"

"Not every morning. But the baby kicks so. And my back hurts if I lie down for too long."

"Alanis had that experience, best I remember. Look, I don't mind your deer-whispering in the wee hours. Just close the porch door."

Suzanne twirled the meadow grass around her finger. "I leave today anyway, so you'll not need to worry about that."

"Alanis mentioned that a room was opening at Rose House."

"I'm not going there after all. I'm just going."

"That's ridiculous. Rose House is a perfectly fine facility, but if you're not comfortable with it, you shouldn't put yourself back on the street."

Suzanne broke the grass and shook it from her fingers. "I told you that I intended to do this on my own. It's what I'm called to do."

"Your St. Francis routine is impressive, but please don't ask me to participate in your Virgin Mary story."

"Besides, I've overstayed my welcome."

"I never said that. Don't use it as an excuse to do what you prefer."

"It's not a matter of preference."

"Anyone in your situation has a right to ask for help. Alanis offered it. You've no cause to leave so far as I'm concerned."

"That's different from being invited to stay with you."

"Alanis invited you, and strange as it seems, she's happier with you here than she was before."

"She would be happier still if she had another child."

"I'm not sure what you're implying. But I'm sure that you don't understand the smallest fraction of what my wife and I have suffered. So please don't offer advice."

"I wasn't advising you. Only making an observation."

In the distance, the deer started and dispersed into the mists.

"Perhaps you're right. It's time for you to go."

Suzanne said nothing but turned toward the house.

Alanis was on the porch, watching them. The meadow glistened between.

6

By midday Suzanne was packed and gone. Alanis pled with her to stay but to no avail. She demanded that Sean go after her. When he refused, she closed herself up in Lily's room.

Sean leaned against the lintel and stared down the hall. This had all happened before. The dust motes danced in shafts of light. Alanis' sobs turned to a wail, a horrible ululating like the mother of the blind boy whom Jackson had killed, like the mothers in his dream as the fire bears down. He covered his ears and shut his eyes until it subsided. Then, in the renewed silence and afternoon sunlight, he noticed that the Buddha was missing from the letter table.

Four months later it returned in a shoebox, along with a handful of Suzanne's effects. A social worker and police officer brought it. Suzanne had died in childbirth, and her infant daughter was currently a ward of the state. The only living relative was an aunt with substance abuse problems who had been deemed unfit to be the child's guardian. The Kilpatricks' address had been scribbled on a paper in Suzanne's wallet, so the social worker decided they should at least be notified, in case they had an interest in the effects or knew about any other kin.

To Sean and Alanis, it was as if their decision was pre-ordained. When the adoption was finalized, they renamed the baby Rose, not Violet, as they had intended to name Lily's sister. She was small but healthy, with thick black hair and fuzz on her shoulders. People who didn't realize that Rose was adopted said that with her features—that hair, those eyes—it was obvious whose child she was.

Open Hand
(Portrait of CER in Four Scenes)

Looking In
(Belle Mead, NJ, 1973)

They lie down in the pea patch to get closer to the dozens of ladybugs, orange, yellow, red and black, or as their heroine Anne Shirley of Green Gables might say, tangerine, sunlight on the pond's surface, drops of blood and chocolate. Girls, six and seven-and-a-half, the youngest freckled and red-haired, the oldest a blonde page boy, both nearly filled with secrets but growing, so there will be room inside them for more, as there always seems to be outside them, space, under the full sun of July afternoons. Each ladybug, known only to them, spiraling sunward like tiny kites and sometimes coming to rest on the blonde or ruddy meadow of their arms, and then no longer like kites but like painted turtles in tall grass trundling awkwardly and disoriented, or like small packages still and self-enclosed, though in both cases what is held inside is delicate and uncertain and closely kept.

It is like what my mother held. In the black-and-white photograph, she, in a sunbonnet, perhaps she is two years old, perches on my grandfather's knee. My grandmother kneels behind, her lips are thickly painted, it must be Sunday, her pleasant gaze betraying nothing more. Unlike his: dark under a severe brow, Heathcliff, but not without a glint of what might be called joy. This is before his right arm was shredded by a silage machine, the arm that almost embraces my mother, who is staring at her hand closed lightly on something we cannot see.

Seeing Out
(Peggy's Cove, NS, 1996)

There we achieved absolute clarity: on a northern shore, where it was far too brisk for July, and the salt wind cut cold into the stones, glacier detritus, that glistened, sun-blinding, and shielded us from the distant barrier beyond which we were not meant to wander, and suddenly we were completely involved in each other down in the bosom of so ancient a pile, washed by the Atlantic. At a distance we were an aspect of the rockface like the cormorants, the gulls, the thousand barnacles feeding, producing, calcifying, none of which we were aware, as I kissed the salt from your cheek and the stones scraped my knees, and the gulls, that I could not see but, in recollection, place above us, drifted, searching.

After, you said, "Here you can see out. The trees are much shorter. There is less in the way between us and the horizon." Near the shore, low-bush blueberries, plentiful and close to the ground, sweeter besides than the high-bush variety down South. Then wide swaths of weedless earth, aspen groves without vines, their double-jointed leaves flickering.

Going Back
(Charlottesville, VA, 2003)

Rereading a long novel is like revisiting a great house. A noise that you hear this time—faintly, and yet you're sure of it—carries you to a passageway, past the gilt-edged portrait that must have been there before (and how did you not see it?), into a bright parlor lit by the mid-winter sun and filled with objects, which you allow to distract you, because novels are spacious and generous, and the noise has proven to be a young lady singing.

When you come to the end of the novel, the second hand ticks onward past the hour's arrival. Always there is another mark ahead of the second hand: potential, a rationale for optimism, as in the final chapters that you flip back to and re-read, which you will always do after the end.

Taking In
(Kingston, NY, 2008)

Take that young girl in, the one whose mother died, whose father died, whose grandmother has only so much left for her, the girl who lies to you and sings to you, who will not eat your food but admires the ritual of your meal times. You carefully untwist the knots of her long, dirty hair. Ubi caritas et amor Deus ibi est, there, combing out the nits, scrubbing the dirt from the cracks in her feet.

Caritas. It is not fastidious. It is not deterred by the urinary stench of unwashed bodies. It does not grow bored by tedious accounts of unfairness and failure. It rarely doubts, it never glances at the clock, it doesn't lock doors. It will say yes too often. It is a harbor, deep and undefended. It keeps its confidences. It is an open hand.

Raking

"After the leaves have fallen, we return
To a plain sense of things…" Wallace Stevens

Except that what falls must be removed, which takes us until spring, because winter comes so soon and buries the last maple leaves in snow, while the oak holds on, staggering and stupefied by December's hard fists, the ground slowly rising around it: a layer of autumn, sheeted in ice, then a scatter of twigs, like small animal bones, and whatever the oak finally lets go of, then snow pack, such that the resulting striations tell a story—temporarily legible, though not plain—that the floods of April begin to uncover before we return to our raking.

Blackbirds descend, a forensics detail on the marshy ground, and preparing to go out among them, I watch from the window by the woodstove while the morning dampness seeps into the creosote, loosening a fragrance that summons the winter, its fading effects, as when I open a book, its dust scrim dispersing, and I cannot remember the plot or even the name of a character but am recalled to a mood it once evoked.

You enter, having just washed your hair, combing through the tangles, moving between me and the window, gathering damp threads tenacious as spider's web between your fingers, smelling of shampoo, and in the glass your reflection, streaked by melting frost, hovers ghostly and intangible.

You look beyond the open blinds through your reflection at the cluttered lawn, and I want to brush aside all that is in the way, to touch you, but such plainness requires resolve, a change of season, the certain risk of a simple sentence.

Crowding Onto the B at 125th Street While Listening to Coltrane Play "Spiral"

Think of paramecia in a circle of light, before the droplet dries out, or bumper cars in a corral, the surge, contact, reversal, contact, until the carny breaks the circuit, that steady flow of juice across flapping sheet metal tongues.

Upon reflection there may be a pattern.

Imagine for instance a triangle described by a redstart's frenetic movements among the following three points: hemlock branch, stone and rotting birch trunk (where the comma symbolizes an intermediate perch along line AB). Fitful, the bird stops to fan his orange feathers like the crazy man with the rosaries who touches all the corners uptown. You and I are still as we watch from behind the hemlock. But something sends the redstart elsewhere.

On second thought there may only be points of departure.

Take the ladder: a series of squares one ascends for clarity. Up there it's all blue. Sometimes, as now, a crow crosses the final frame and becomes the whole picture. You pause to watch her exit.

Funneled in, spiraling out: the function of accidentals is alertness to the beauty of resolution, just as the rationale for climbing is flight.

Conversation with a Sparrow in Lockeport, Nova Scotia

"I can see that you're disappointed."

    "I'm sorry. It's just that we came all this

    distance and, I admit, I hoped for something uncommon."

"I didn't startle and fly away."

    "Yes, and I'm grateful."

"I chirped for several seconds till you found me."

    "I do appreciate that, and that you perched

    among azalea blossoms."

"But you would have moved on, indifferent, if you had

known I was only a sparrow."

    "Is it a moral failing to seek the unusual?"

"Can you name, with confidence, my species?"

    "Fair enough. Even when I try, I cannot retain

    details. Peterson has pages and pages of sparrows."

"Who all look the same, like stars and grains of sand? Your

scale is too vast. Am I not the only sparrow you've
encountered today?"

"The only one I've actually listened to."
"And when I fly from here to the hemlock, singing along the
way,
how little will you have understood?"

"I take your point, sparrow, but I sought surprise, not
erudition."
"You came for color, not knowledge or empathy."

"If I return to my den and learn all there is to
know
about sparrows of your kind, what, truly, will
come of it?"
"Nothing, perhaps. But if you would avoid
disappointment,
bathe in the dust when it's dusty."

"That will be more difficult for me than for a drab
little bird."

Coda

("There are no loons")

"Yes, but try to enjoy the gulls.

Seriously, how often are you close to so very many?

Ring-billed.

They're smaller than the ones we're used to.

Those yellowy legs,

The way that one perched on the post,

How his feathers splurge

up in the breeze.

I suppose that's not his tail feathers

but his wing tips that are ink-dipped?

You see it when they fly.

Go ahead, try to identify that sparrow.

I'll sit here in the car and appreciate the gulls."

Who Killed Cock Robin?

First I ran past a shredded McDonald's bag, ketchup packets spattering the pavement.

Next came squirrel remains, also shredded but strangely bloodless. These I dodged.

Then, up ahead, there were two crows in the road. X marks the spot. At three paces, the crows flew, and I paused. A robin lay on its back, legs stiff and splayed, red breast speckled white where the crows had begun their plucking.

On the grassy curb next to it, there was a dollar.

A quarter of a mile farther on, another robin lay in the road. Dignity had not yet abandoned it. Surrounded by space and quiet, it was a fallen soldier. Its eyes were covered with felted lids. In short order, I thought, there will be crows. I considered scooping it up and putting it in my sweatshirt pocket, but thought better of it. I looked around for a dollar.

Who killed cock robin?

A band of marauding suburban boys with BB guns? Too early in the morning. Old age? The coincidence of both robins having died of natural causes would be uncanny. Lawn chemicals tainting the earthworms? Perhaps. This world is laced with death.

Later the same day, one that moralizing forecasters called "excessively hot," I was uptown walking the dog (she was panting in the heat) and passed a man who was frantically rifling through his pockets and backpack. He seemed to be carrying all he owned, and he did not own much. Before long, he sprinted by me, startling the dog, who tugged me over to a dollar on the sidewalk. It was folded and faded. Had the backpacked man dropped it? Had he dropped another by poor cock robin earlier in the day? He paused near a planter ahead of us. I picked up the dollar and decided to ask him. Again, he was searching his pockets angrily, and then like Alice's rabbit, he sprinted several yards down the sidewalk, as if suddenly remembering he was late. Once more he stopped, so I did, too, to watch him. He seemed to be rearranging things compulsively, moving bits of this and that from one pocket to another and to his backpack. Although he was flustered, he had a system, hip pocket-backpack-shirt pocket, shaky and hurling forward and yet evidently in a loop. Predictably, he took off, this time around the bend.

Unable to catch him, unsure that I wanted to, I decided that the dollar, now in my pocket, should be donated to charity. It was not mine, after all. I should not spend it on coffee, for instance, and thereby feed my head on the backs of underpaid Latin American farm workers and my back-packed stranger. I should give it to a righteous cause.

Six weeks later the dollar was still with me, mysteriously increasing in value the longer it lingered, like the question of how the robins died. "It's only a dollar," I would think, knowing it had become more than that. It was a pocket al-batross. I could not seem to get rid of it. It might have been a tattoo for all its persistence on my person. Actually, nei-ther of those metaphors—neither albatross nor tattoo—is adequate. For the dollar was inside, always hidden, unno-ticed except by me, whom it nagged like a stitch or cramp. I intended it for one of those ASPCA jars that, until now, I seemed to find at every diner and deli counter. Had there been an up-tick in the humane treatment of stray cats and pit bulls? For all those jars seemed to have disappeared from our town. Meanwhile robins were dying in our streets, the collateral damage of our insistence on verdant lawns.

What better explanation than that for who killed cock robin—two of them, in fact?

I began to wonder if I had passed the same robin twice. Had I been going in circles, unwittingly? Reach into your waistcoat pocket and look at your watch. The seconds fall off along a circle that is also the straight line of time. All forward motion is circular, an ellipse fractured with ellipses, like the paths of my backpacked stranger. That could be comforting, moving forward but regularly revisiting familiar spaces, a delightful circularity, like a merry-go-round, the one you rode as a child, your mother disappearing and returning to sight, your point of origin and return. Imagine a plastic robin's nest, three seats, each a bright blue egg cracked open. You, your best friend, and an unidentified blonde girl who reminds you of the youngest Partridge family daughter are the nestlings. You are surrounded by mallards, swans, a toucan. There are no ponies or stallions on this carousel, for that is not our theme. Sparrows and pigeons bus the ground around the line of waiting children. Your mother waves each time you pass.

That is not the carnival ride of the backpacked stranger. In Hitchcock's *Strangers on a Train*, a murderer is killed when a carousel spins out of control and crushes him. He is chasing down his partner, who had a change of heart about following through on his role in a homicidal pact. That black-and-white image of men creeping around the merry-go-round, the camera always angled so that we tip forward or backward, unsure of our footing and spinning quickly toward chaos: isn't that a closer analogy to my backpacked stranger's obsessive-compulsive rearrangements? In the moment that he stops and digs into his pockets, something is distressingly out of place. The lighter should be in the left pocket, the receipts in the shirt pocket behind the cigarettes, the good luck buckeye and crucifix glow if misplaced, they become hot, they'll burn through the zipped-up side pocket of the backpack because they do not belong there.

If a bird in the hand is worth two in the bush, what is the value of one dead robin in a pocket (had I been so bold as to pick it up) versus two on the road for poets to contemplate and crows to sup on? Go back to the first scene, the robin's body, plucked and broken. I don't now how you died, and the question has become by turns crucial and comical, an absurd responsibility, like making sense of each day when there may be no sense to any of this. Kneeling on the ground beside you, I am emptying my pockets, a clown, whose pockets never empty.

Writing about his travels on the Kona coast of Hawaii, Robert Louis Stevenson reported that the indigenous people were awed by pockets. Over a century earlier, Cook's men had experienced this, too. Their clothes were perceived to be part of their bodies. Reaching into a pocket, these explorers performed a bloodless evisceration, the harvesting of internal treasures to present to their newfound friends. This is not far-fetched. How attached am I to my wallet and keys? Nearly as viscerally as to my spleen, more so than to my appendix. Extend that sense of the essential to encompass all the contents of one's pockets, and consider what I have done to our backpacked man by pocketing his dollar: a veritable transplant from an unwilling donor. How could I imagine that re-gifting this vital organ to the ASPCA would break my connection and absolve me of my responsibility? At least the crows had the grace to harvest organs only after their robin was dead.

Six weeks passed, as I've said, with the dollar in my pocket—or more accurately moving from one trouser pocket to the next, along with my keys, an eraser, and the small creek stone I've carried for decades. It was handed to me at a baptism, I pocketed it, and there it has remained, symbolic of what? It could not be tossed aside, so it kept company with my stranger's dollar. One evening, before I went off to teach *Jane Eyre*, I needed coffee. The can in the office was empty. There was a café nearby, and I had two dollars, but one, as you know, was earmarked. Desperate for caffeine, I settled for tea. I lowered the pouches—two, for maximum strength—slowly into a cup of hot water and waited for all the tea to leach out. It was strangely quiet. The window of the office kitchenette was so airtight that the trees outside, gesturing ecstatically at the approaching storm, were soundless. Crows, a cloud of them, spilled from the wind above and around the trees. If they cawed, I could not hear them. I placed my ear to the cool glass. How thick must it be that not even a thunderhead of crows rattles it? Two of the birds broke off, black rain drops, and splashed onto the paved driveway beyond the trees. I pried up the sash.

"We've come for the robin," declared the largest.

"You're too late," I replied. "Another pair beat you to him."

"Then you'll kindly refund our deposit," the second said and opened his bill like a money clip.

Closing the window, I fumbled with the dollar, switched it from my right pocket to my left, and returned to *Jane Eyre* with my cup of tea.

The self-important, hypocritical Mr. Brocklehurst quizzes his prospective pupil, Jane, about the nature of humility. He brags that his daughter, Augusta, has visited his charity school and marveled at the girls, who are "quiet and plain…with their hair combed behind their ears, and their long pinafores, and those little Holland pockets outside their frocks…" At best, those pockets would hold the girls' piecework. Surely the pockets contain nothing personal, nothing that would create a bulge and signify ownership, possessiveness, wealth. Such an impregnated pocket could keep a girl from passing through the eye of a needle into the kingdom of heaven.

Jane fails the quiz, and we admire her failure because we know that she intimately understands humility, unlike her pompous instructor. She is an independent and fiery orphan, whose free hand for the least of these, despite her own neediness, is evident when she gives her breakfast roll to a robin. This happens just before the descent of Brocklehurst. At the window of her room, Jane has indifferently watched his carriage arrive, when she spies the hungry bird, "on the twigs of the leafless cherry-tree nailed against the wall near the casement." We watch Jane anxiously as she struggles to open the sash and rushes to feed the robin before her nurse catches her. We are to admire the imprudence of true charity.

Now is the moment for me to confess, reader, that I did not donate the dollar. That very night on the way to class, I spent it on coffee, the tea having (as I anticipated) nothing like the boost I needed to teach in the evening. Rationalizing, I could point out that I have subsequently given many other dollars to good causes, that one of those dollars could, in essence, be construed as having belonged to my backpacked stranger, assuming any dollar ever did. Be that as it may, the neatly folded dollar from the sidewalk, coupled with a second of my own, fed my habit, not a stranger or a robin or a crow.

What killed the robins?

These divagations: are they bringing us any closer to the answer? I have, as always, plunged my hands into my pockets and moved on quickly, only glancing at you as you insist that I come to the point. I turn the stone over and over in my hand for reassurance that something bright, sonorous, and worth noticing develops as more robins crowd the page. But perhaps that is an artful dodge, an excuse to make much of a small thing, or to make little of all this. I should take a pen from my pocket and scratch out an answer on the back of the dollar bill, had I not spent it. The backpacked stranger would leave his circuit and go off on a tangent toward a bus that would plunge him into invisibility, the city's heart. I would look you in the eye and say, "We go no further," and you would douse the torch that has dimly lit our way.

Fine. Then later, in the dark, a voice might say, "Who killed Cock Robin?"

"I," said the sparrow, "with my bow and arrow, I killed Cock Robin."

"Who saw him die?"

"I," said the Fly, "with my little eye, I saw him die."

So Fly was a witness. Fish, we soon learn, caught the blood, suggesting that the slaying was ritualistic. The rest of the animal kingdom participated in an elaborate funeral. Answer the following questions to demonstrate your comprehension of this English rhyme:

Who made the shroud?

Why might a Dove be an appropriate choice for a mourner?

What is implied by the plural pronoun "We" in the Wren's response?

Bonus: The Linnet volunteers to fetch and carry the "link." What is a link in this context?

Since spending the dollar, I have seen my backpacked stranger again. An ellipse that takes in the uptown Trailways terminal is his halting merry-go-round. This time, and next, and the time after, he asked me for a light, because he has always misplaced not a dollar but a lighter. Bics and their disposable offspring, the whole Crayola rainbow like unfound plastic Easter eggs, nestle in the sickly grass along the sidewalks of our dirty city. Some were discarded when empty, tossed on the ground along with candy wrappers, soda lids, and crack pipes. Some fell out accidentally, fledglings, full of potential: the stranger's lighter during a round of rearrangement. Now he is forever without, though each time he turns a corner he forgets that the lighter has gone missing.

It found another use. The linnet, a poet's fowl (though not quite a nightingale or lark, the former being too elevated for "Who Killed Cock Robin," the latter rhyming his way into the position of clerk), made it his link, to light the poor robin's way to dusty death.

Lines Written at the Cleanup from Hurricane Irene

The Scoharie filled the church basement with mud and eels,
Submerged the pews and rose to the sills of the stained-glass
windows,
Seeped into the fire-proof safe, defaced its contents,
The traces of a past.

                         As if to go the creek one better,
After the flood we tore out the sheetrock, but with heart and
design.
We wore dust masks, swung crow bars, and joked,
"There's nothing stashed in the walls, no silver dollars
Skimmed from the offering, no relics of Methodist martyrs
Or Presbyterian heretics."

                    From the basement
Emerged the wise men, soiled but salvageable.
When there's a lawn again, they'll re-attend the nativity,
Pending the recovery of a Christ child.

Almost Easter

Turning over stones that lined the tulip beds, my son re-animates two salamanders, whose path from dormancy to urgency is black lightning, a photo negative, except that on their backs they bear embers. A baseball, in the Orioles' colors, lost last autumn after the maple dropped its leaves, presents itself at the same time, as if to buy the salamanders precious seconds to preserve their liberty. "This is going too far," I think, "next I'll say there is a little girl in a sundress, who is peeling a tangerine," and there is not, although on a branch above, a robin presides, Atropos, shear-beaked. On this day what follows is as undecided as it is bright, a paradox that won't be borne at the end of things, as depicted in the mosaics at Santa Maria Assunta in Torcello, where rich Venetian merchants bob in flames, stoked by the long staffs of unremarkable angels, who are outclassed by an assortment of gallivanting demons, winged, blue, yanking hair and beards to add humiliation because pain without insult would be ennobling, or might be thought so, and such thinking has no place in a proper hell.

Kindertotenlieder

Aubade II

(For Elizabeth Bishop at 100)

At Lockeport the children rose early
To search for urchins, sand dollars, and shrimp
In the tidal pools placed by the moon
Before dawn, like gift boxes, among the stones
Tumbled here by a glacier, its frozen palm
Imprinted, it seems, on their cold surface
Where I sit, minding my son,
Nimble scrambler, and watch the scoters

That bob between the rough surf and the fog,
Persistent, looking for food,
Their feathers shellacked in salted dampness,
The sea, a penetrating "transmutation of fire,"
Their cold providence. It's a keener search
Than hardship can deter. As a lobsterman told me,
"You don't really think about it's hard,
Because you're there to get what you need."

The ducks watch and plunge, while the sunrise
Peels fog from the nearby stones and mats of kelp.
Brightening, Jacob kneels close to a pool.
He is joined by my niece, in knee socks,
Remarkable finder, her yellow bucket
Ready to receive. She too kneels close,
Inspecting, expectant eyes of the gods
To this briny enclosure, its creatures

Multitudinous, tracking in all directions,
Seeking and being sought, so much
Like the rest of us, living and
Searching being synonymous.
Jacob lifts a shell and hails me.
He and his cousin will never tire of this,
All the life in the pools, every find
Suggesting another, the potential, the hope.

On the Burning Deck

The red-haired boy sings "Red River Valley," solo, in the junior high recital. Wearing a white Oxford and spring pastel tie, he sings with his eyes closed, his nerves dancing on the surface of his lids, his arms stiff by his side. "He is far more courageous than I ever was," I think. Everyone cheers for him, though vocal music is clearly not his strong suit. The junior high recital rewards effort. No one seems to expect to be charmed by a new tenor voice, let alone impressed by his promising technical skill. For the entire evening, earnestness is all: "Danny Boy" in the sincere, small voice of a girl in a pinafore; "The British Grenadiers" rendered by a towering boy with a baby face; "Don't Cry For Me Argentina" struggling to be heard over the loudly meandering accompaniment. Most violins almost strike the note, most cellos rise from guttural muttering to tentative warbling. After each performance, there are hugs and high fives.

Because students need a critique of the quality of their work, it's not enough to reward courage or appraise effort. Most of us have been told "Good Job!" when we knew otherwise and needed more than a pat on the back to move forward. But for the shy and earnest, the modest and intelligent, stepping up to the microphone is not simply a matter of cold palms and mild nausea; for nearly all students, shy and bold alike, most school performances are compelled, the content prescribed. Consider the case of that brilliant, shy poet, Elizabeth Bishop, whose painful modesty and need of privacy are reflected in the way she imagines a schoolboy reciting a poem and being in love. "Love's the boy stood on the burning deck," she declares, "trying to recite 'The boy stood on/the burning deck…'"

Bishop's burning boy stood first on a deck of the English Romantic poet Felicia Hemans' imagining. Hemans based her "Casabianca" on a legend that during the Battle of the Nile, the young child of Commodore Casabianca followed orders and remained at his post on board the French warship *L'Orient* while the vessel burned around him. In Hemans' poem, he pleads with his father to be allowed to stand down, but his father "faint in death below" cannot hear him. The ship explodes, and the "noblest thing that perished there" was the boy's "faithful heart." For over a century, "Casabianca" was a memory gem, and when it wasn't being dutifully recited by English and American school children, it was being parodied by critics. The boy stood on the burning deck/He'd best jump off and save his neck. Long after Hemans had been forgotten, "the boy stood on the burning deck" remained seared onto school-children's minds, an example of filial piety that surely more than one child questioned, if only in secret as he dutifully recited the lines. The boy flamed out with the demise of recitation as an instructional strategy, but not before the 1910s, when Elizabeth Bishop encountered him, perhaps in her McGuffey's Reader.

Love goes down with the ship. It's possible that to a young person, the boy's noble deed and anxious plea aren't entirely silly. Adolescent love, in particular, watches himself going down with the ship. Sure that his suffering is immeasurable, even unprecedented, he draws some comfort from imagining all those friends and enemies who will recall his tragic persistence and recite his virtues in bathetic, mournful lines. For the shy child on the burning deck, adolescence must therefore be peculiarly alienating. She would gladly remain quietly offstage, but she would also have her ideas admired and her life count for something. She would be fully accepted without being singled out to perform a role not of her choosing. Critics have argued that Bishop's "Casabianca" subtly registers the challenges that she faced as a lesbian who navigated heteronormative spaces and as a poet who didn't want gender to constrain her reception. Her boy—love—stands "stammering elocution," feeling one thing, publicly staging another, and struggling to reconcile the two. Love's obstinate, ineloquent, and conflicted. Love's the burning boy.

At the junior high recital, a trio is tuning. One girl, her hair in complex, colorful weaves, cannot face the audience. She bows her instrument so lightly that the notes won't sound. She shrugs often, as if there's nothing to be done about this, or as if it's of no consequence anyway. She sighs and keeps her back turned. If it truly didn't matter, she might spin around, step forward, and screech away blithely as a starling. She might, that is, perform a role, rather than be herself under scrutiny and duress. As it is, she cares enough to be paralyzed by embarrassment, unable to stammer boldly or leap off the deck. Afterwards she gives no one a high five.

Hemans and her burning boy were resurrected in the early 1990s. I was there when the wreckage resurfaced. Like many aspiring scholars at that time, I wanted to understand why Hemans and comparable poets were difficult to read in the ways we had been taught. I had a moment of clarity when my wife and I visited her great uncle, who had been a grammar school student in the same years as Bishop. He had made his living as a violinist in a small orchestra, and now that he was semi-retired, he spent much of the day in his flower gardens. He was an expert on daylilies. Having lived long and been curious about many things, he knew how to make two young people feel as though they were interesting. When he asked what poets I was researching, I sheepishly answered that they were an obscure lot. "Felicia Hemans, for instance," I said. Without a single stammer, he recited "Casabianca," then went on to "The Sandpiper." The second poem was by a New England poet, Celia Thaxter, but the confusion was illuminating. For Thaxter and Hemans shared a language of sensibility expressed in accessible, affecting forms; poems such as "Casabianca" were only "superficially superficial," as Kingsley Amis once said of another Hemans recitation favorite, "Graves of a Household." Bishop picks up on this—the foolishness and pathetic beauty of the poem, its refusal to let go of the child who memorized it even after she can see through its shimmering surface. Caroline's uncle talked about having to "get those poems by heart" as a child. I wondered about that phrase. I suspect that for some schoolchildren, memorizing "Casabianca" was all mind, and only on the surface of the mind at that. Reciting it was a "performance" as we apply that term to a Chevy as opposed to an Ian McKellan. For Caroline's uncle, however, the heart seems really to have been involved, much as Hemans' was when she imagined the child at his post. For this elderly violinist, advanced years and a capacity for irony could not displace a poem gotten by heart.

"Come and sit by my side if you love me/Do not has-ten to bid me adieu." I watch the red-haired boy standing on a burning deck and singing. Or because this is a cowboy song, he's on a prancing Appaloosa and the flames are the sunset. Either way he is center stage against his will, but he's given himself over to the attempt. It's a set piece of the junior high music class recital, and parents are expected to tear up and snap photos, just as siblings are meant to squirm and roll their eyes. Much of this is superficial, and yet it starts to get to you. You try to be cool and objec-tive, but there he is, your son, doing his duty, singing that silly love ballad as if Gene Autry himself were judging. All the young dudes, even his brother, are quiet and watchful, because they have been on deck or will be soon enough. Love's the burning boy, and all you can think is "I love this child" even though you risk the embarrassment of a tear. It could be worse. The audience could start singing along, the way the Austrians begin to sing "Edelweiss" with Father Von Trapp in *The Sound of Music*. Then they *are* all singing along, and you are, too. It's a conflagration. The masts are down. The hull's taking in the sea by the gallons. We might as well all be on the burning deck together. It's likely that we already are, whether or not we want to be. There's nothing for it but to sing.

"N.B. Deer in Gowbarrow Park like skeletons"

Look like, not enjoy.
"Vultures like skeletons":
Sometimes it works both ways.

N.B. Don't settle for clever.

His sister would not lose the deer for the daffodils.
Forever his sister, like,
Like you as in "enjoy you,"
Love may be too strong.

Loneliness is not a cloud.
Deer skeletons among the flowers.

— Note: The title is the last line of Dorothy Wordsworth's
journal entry for 15 April 1802, the source of her brother's
"I wandered lonely as a cloud."

Wanton Boys

Yellow jackets dandle on ripened pears.

        Shoot them off with a BB gun.

Tent caterpillars shroud blossoming peach trees.

        Incinerate them with a magnifying glass.

House flies swarm the cider press mash.

        Shoo and swat them in flight.

Meal worms bore into the corn flour sacks.

        Drown black beetles in the cow trough.

Potato bugs gnaw away the leaves of young plants.

        Gather them in sandwich bags and run them over
with a bicycle.

Corn worms burrow in the silver queen ears.

        Pinch them headless when you shuck.

Locusts sway from the oaten beards.

        Bat them across the fence line with a Louisville
Slugger.

Bruise

When Arnold beat his children, he allowed his mind to wander. He paused for dramatic effect. He anticipated the poker game or checked his phone messages. The youngest ones—Buggy, who spent most days with Aunt Flo, and Chester, before he died in the fire—never seemed to learn the difference between a breather and a sigh of contentment, a pause and a full stop. No matter how often Lorna advised them not to move or they'd get it double, if Arnold took out his phone, Buggy and Chester would let their shoulders drop and exhale. It was like blowing on live coals. As Arnold's ring-studded backhand swiftly responded, Lorna would shake her head and make her plans.

Not that Lorna was plotting to run away from home or kill her father, although murdering him in a story such as this would likely be pardonable, and for her it would be simple. Arnold usually slept in the recliner in front of the TV after assailing his children, his mouth gaping open, snoring. Lorna knew about jugular veins, owned a sharp pen knife, and was not repulsed by blood. Although she was guilty of having imagined this method of liberating herself and her brothers, she would never act on it. For Lorna was a high-road, narrow-path girl. She had decided that it was her own moral failing to wish Arnold were dead by any other than natural causes. And as difficult as it was to conceive of a plan for reforming him, Lorna made that her problem to solve. She and her brothers would stay put, and her father would change.

It may come as a surprise to you that Arnold had not been beaten as a child. His mother, a wan, silent woman who worked at the Fluff and Fold and whom everyone called "retarded" right in front of her as if she were deaf or it just didn't matter, died of a heart attack when Arnold was twelve. His father's violence was confined to his cellmates in the penitentiary, where he'd been sent just before Arnold's birth, and it was stopped abruptly when a prison guard, who had had a belly full of his swaggering and racial slurs, looked away as a handful of inmates kicked him into the next kingdom. No one ever laid a hand on Arnold in love or anger. The woman he called Grandma let him stay on her sofa and eat whatever the rest of the house was having until she caught him naked in the broom closet with the one she called her daughter. You could say she kicked him out, but no boots were involved. She just said, "Go," and he left.

You may of course find in that bleak childhood an explanation for Arnold's abusiveness as a grown-up, and that's why Lorna thought a reform strategy should be attempted. He was a result of nurture, or lack of it, not nature, she concluded. Not that she knew as much as you do about his growing up—only that his parents died when he was young, and he'd been on the streets at sixteen. It was enough to give her reason to promise Buggy and Chester that their father would change in time. Chester doubted it openly. Buggy looked up to Lorna and trusted her, and when he was old enough to question her judgment, he didn't, except in the privacy of his own mind, and indirectly even there. So fifteen years later, after Buggy and Lorna thought Arnold had changed, but Arnold shoved Buggy against the wall for smirking, Buggy erupted in a fit of violent anger that made even *their* house blanch.

No matter how impossible their father became, Lorna would not endorse running away. Chester often pleaded for it, and occasionally she did finagle temporary retreats to Aunt Flo's house down the street. Aunt Flo was not a blood relation but a sympathetic neighbor. A diabetic, her legs were so swollen that she could not answer the door when Lorna knocked. The knock was a mere courtesy anyway. They could just walk in anytime. Flo collected stray cats as well as abused children, and if her apartment reeked of the dozens of cat food tins scattered around it, browned and crisped by the overworked radiators, it smelled like sleep to Lorna and her brothers. That is, unless Darius was around. Flo's son was a junkie, who came home periodically to get fed and shower and steal the cash his mother left for him. That was the pity of it. Flo put cash in the freezer knowing that he would go after it when she slept but hoping he'd just ask her for it for once. Instead he pretended to be clean and doing fine on his wages from sweeping the Regal between shows. He may have been harmless, but Lorna didn't trust how he watched her when she brought the kids over. He stared and chewed his thumbnail. It made her uneasy that she couldn't read him.

Not the way she could read Arnold. She knew when he was dangerous. His signs were as follows:

1) Silence: Arnold was a noisy man, a chatterer and hummer who kept the TV and radio blaring. If the house was quiet, proceed with caution.

2) Sobriety: Drunkenness mellowed Arnold. A thin man, though strong, he became sleepy after two quick Schaefers, which he regularly downed when he returned from work. He never beat his children after his beers.

3) The Crown: This was a yellow sweatband that Arnold kept in his hip pocket. He did not always don it before a beating, but if it was on, take cover. He grew darker and seemed to swell beneath it.

Once, the crown dropped from his pocket when he was putting the garbage on the snow bank out front. For half an hour, it lay there, an old banana peel, ready to go out with the rest of the trash. Lorna stared at it while she ate her breakfast of corn chips. Without his crown, does a tyrant have power? A squirrel slinked up the mound of garbage bags and began to plunder. Beer cans, an actual banana peel, and coffee grounds spilled around the crown. Lorna fingered her chips and watched. Suddenly there was a sharp crack, and the squirrel's right side exploded into blood and viscera. "Were you just gonna set there and watch him make more work for me, Lorna?" Arnold asked, tossed his pistol onto the table, and strode out to the pile. He left the mess for Lorna but retrieved his crown.

Lorna was questioned by the nurse that day about the welt on her cheek. "Chester smacked me with the butt of his cap gun," she said. It was a brilliant lie. Lorna was ingenious at covering her father's traces, but she rarely had to lie outright. Arnold usually hit his children where it wouldn't show.

Where is Lorna's mother in this story, you wonder? Shortly after Buggy turned two years old, there was a knock at the door on a Sunday morning. It was a tall man with green eyes and a moustache. He wore a suit like a preacher. "Where's Suzanne?" he asked. One of his eyeteeth was capped silver. "She ain't awake yet," Lorna said, and it may have been true, because neither she nor Arnold had come home since the Friday fight, when Arnold chased her with his belt, and she hit him in the face with the cactus that Chester had gotten from Aunt Flo for Christmas. "Okay, you tell her that her brother Jim paid a visit," he said, winked at Lorna, and left. Suzanne had no living brothers, Lorna knew that much. But when Arnold returned, and her mother never did, Lorna concluded that whoever he was, the green-eyed preacher had tracked her down and rescued her. He had left his church behind and gone off to sea with her mama. She envisioned them sailing toward a land of blue mountains. Lorna mentioned the preacher to no one, not even Aunt Flo. Sad as she was that her mother had left, she didn't want to put her escape at risk. Who, besides Arnold, could blame her mother for running off? "Let her try to come back in my house and take my kids, negligent bitch," he'd declare, twisting his crown between his two hard hands. Even now, when Lorna had determined that she and her brothers would never run away, because they were right and her father was wrong, she did not begrudge her mother's seizing the moment. She would not think about why her mother hadn't come back for them, secretly, in the night.

I have mentioned Arnold's rings. There were three: his high school class ring, his Coast Guard ring, and the bowling league all-area ring for the year that Sanitation went all the way. He never removed them. When he watched TV, he turned them constantly, like little dials. Each contained a different color of stone, and despite their painful role in the beatings, Lorna admired them. She did not often seek conversation with her father, but she had once asked about the Coast Guard ring. "Spent two years fishing wetbacks out of the ocean in Florida. Would've been happy to do it for the rest of my life, except your mama missed the snow, god knows why. Biggest mistake of my life, leaving the service. What did coming back here get me?"

Lorna wondered why he didn't abandon them, instead of hitting them, and go back to Florida. Aside from the two Schaefers per day and reruns of *Magnum P.I.*, his only daily pleasure seemed to be the shower, where he spent a half hour every evening after work. He was nothing if not clean. He hated his job, which primarily consisted of maintaining Lewisburg's degraded sewer lines. "It's a good day when I ain't spent more than half of it in someone else's shit," he would swear, daring Chester or Lorna to complain about school. Although he worked, unlike most of the men on her street, he never seemed to have any money, which Darius said was because her father couldn't so much as take a piss without placing a bet on it. Mr. Sinja's Deli on the corner sold lottery tickets and had a card game in the back every night. The pool hall was by the stop where Arnold got off the bus from work. "He's probably keeping you for collateral when the mafia comes to collect," Darius joked. Lorna figured that her father didn't actually want her and her brothers. It's that he owned them and not much else. He took no pleasure in beating his children. Just reassurance.

One winter evening after Suzanne left, Darius announced that he knew Arnold was a beater. They were at Aunt Flo's, where Arnold's behavior was common knowledge, but no one discussed it. It's impossible to say what prompted Darius, who had come home indefinitely to escape the cold. None of the kids were bruised. Nearly three weeks had passed since Arnold had last raised his hand. Except to take his shower, drink his beer, and open a bag of chips or can of Chef Boyardee for the kids' dinner, he had rarely been home at night. This meant that he was winning at Sinja's and sleeping with the women who watched. On the evening of Darius' announcement, Lorna had taken herself and her brothers to Aunt Flo's to sleep because the heat wouldn't come on in their apartment. It was risky. If her father returned to find them away at Flo's, the three-week streak would surely end. Nonetheless, she had dripped the faucets and hoped he stayed gone till tomorrow.

Flo's place was tropical. Darius was stretched out on the sofa with his shirt off. There was a thin patch of hair on his bony chest that he scratched continuously. Between his hipbones, which jutted out above his beltline, a coral snake was tattooed. "So your old man smacks you around," he called out conclusively, like a lawyer on a police procedural.

The TV is always loud at Aunt Flo's house, and everyone was watching *American Idol*, but there was no ignoring Darius. He repeated himself.

"Now Darius keep your nose out of their business," Aunt Flo called back in a breathless falsetto from the depths of her recliner. The cats on her bosom rearranged themselves.

"Child-beaters is everybody's business," Darius returned in his best Sam Waterston voice. "Reckon a body ought to call CPS."

Lorna cringed. Arnold, she could predict and plan for. Foster care, she could not. "I got everything under control," she said.

Darius scratched. "Don't look like it. Elsewise your apartment wouldn't be cold. He's a beater, and negligent to boot."

Lorna shook her head. "He doesn't beat us."

"He hit Buggy," Chester protested.

Darius laughed. "Ho, Miss Lorna, you gone and perjured yourself. And for what? A sewer-rat kid-beater?"

"You wouldn't say that to his face, you twig," Lorna shot back.

Darius rubbed his chest. "Of course not! I value my

worthless life. But that don't mean what I say ain't true, and CPS ought to know about it." Darius took out his phone.

Aunt Flo muted *American Idol.* "Now Darius put that phone away and take your nose out of their business."

Darius kept his eyes on Lorna as he dialed. "Naw, Mama, it's my civic duty."

Aunt Flo sighed and shook the remote at him. "Now Darius you watch yourself or I may run out of freezer money as well as patience."

Darius checked his messages and looked again at Lorna. His eyes were rheumy and expressionless. He slid the phone back beneath the snake.

"Stop your nonsense," Aunt Flo added as she pumped up the volume of the TV. "I mean to hear this young man sing."

Two nights later, Arnold's luck turned bad. He rounded up his children from Flo's at 2 AM and took them back to the apartment, now warmed by two battery-powered space heaters he'd bought before he lost all his earnings. He was wearing his crown. He intended to make up for lost time.

He began that very night. Chester couldn't find his inhaler, and Flo's cats had brought on his asthma. Arnold smacked the sputum out of him.

Buggy couldn't sleep because the heaters looked like robots, and he was terrified of robots. Arnold explained the irrationality of this by first kicking the robots and then Buggy.

Lorna assumed that she would get hers, since she was responsible for moving them to Flo's. But her father waited, and Lorna tread lightly. It would come, she knew that, but if she were strategic, the duration and severity could be minimized. The night passed, and another day. By Thursday morning, the robots' batteries were dead, and the only food in the house was a can of ravioli. After Arnold left for work, Lorna collected six beer cans from around the house and four more along the street. These were good for fifty cents at Sinja's. Lorna bought a Three Musketeers Bar.

"It's a bit early for chocolate, Miss Lorna?" Mr. Sinja asked.

"Not in our house."

Mrs. Sinja added two overripe bananas to the brown paper bag, claiming that no one would buy them.

Back home, Lorna divided the candy bar and bananas. She swore both boys to secrecy and carried the wrapper, peels, and bag to school with her to throw away. The Sinjas would remain silent since they were implicated. But Arnold found out.

From the time he got home from work, he was silent. His case of Schaefer was empty, so he didn't drink his two beers. He was wearing his crown.

During a commercial break from *Magnum P.I.*, he asked, "Why didn't you eat that can of ravioli for breakfast?"

Lorna had prepared for this. "I figured it was supper," which was the truth.

"You didn't consider I might get us supper on the way home?" He had come home with a loaf of bread and bologna. This would double as breakfast.

"No sir. I mean, I figured we already had supper in the cupboard. The ravioli."

"No, what you had there was breakfast. Don't I provide it? So what did you feed your brothers?"

Lorna hesitated. A tactical error.

"I said don't I provide it?"

"Yes, sir, of course, it's just…"

"Don't you say another word, young lady. Either ya'll didn't eat, or you went begging, which I ain't going to tolerate. Don't I provide? Go in the kitchen and reach me that can of ravioli."

It was when she was stretched up to the cupboard that the first blow landed across her back. She fell against the cabinet.

"Do I let my children go hungry? That's your worthless mother's job. Or maybe you're taking after her?"

The second blow was a backhand—the rings—that swiped Lorna across the side and onto the floor. The third was more of a nudge with his boot heel than a kick, though it came under a torrent of reprimands. Lorna didn't listen to them. She was concentrating on putting her mind outside the apartment. This is what you did during a beating, she had learned: don't appear to relax, but put your mind elsewhere. Out the front gate, for instance. When you opened it, the wire hinge squeaked. She thought how it sounded like the Guinea pig in Miss Du Bois' Kindergarten years ago. Anytime a kid crumbled his sandwich bag, Elmo would squeak with excitement because he associated the sound with his food sack. Just the way she associated the sound of the front gate with the Guinea pig.

The screen door slapped shut.

Lorna could not see what followed because she was too dazed and breathless to move. Darius had come over on a mission from Aunt Flo. Buggy, who always stayed with her while Chester and Lorna were at school, had left his blanket. When Darius swung open the gate, Arnold had just paused to check his phone. The squeak brought him to the door, but not before Darius had seen Lorna crumpled on the ground. Darius turned and ran, dialing the police, but within two blocks Arnold caught him, pinned him to a wall, latched onto his groin, and made it clear to him what the story needed to be when the cops traced his phone unless he wanted his genitals fed to him. This is why the police ended up at Aunt Flo's instead of Arnold's and Darius ended up overnight in jail for prank calling 9-1-1.

Lorna stayed home from school the next day because it hurt to breathe too deeply. Arnold disappeared for the weekend, but left the cupboard well stocked. From the couch

Lorna coached Chester in how to prepare Ramen noodles, fry canned salmon patties, and heat peas. For dessert they had Dolly Madison banana cupcakes. Lorna had read the signs: they were to indulge, and their father would keep his distance. It was not an apology, but something like an acknowledgement of having crossed a boundary. Lorna and her brothers slept without worry for two days, despite the cold.

In her convalescence, Lorna decided that it was time to speed up the implementation of her plan to reform her father. She could act on two strategies immediately:

1) Ensure a constant supply of beer: Lorna would see to it that her father had his two per day under all circumstances. She would speak to Darius about hiding an emergency stash for the rare occasion, as on Thursday, when Arnold hadn't replenished his empty case right away. Creepy as he was, Darius seemed to want to help. There were two risks—first, that her father would surely realize that his empty case had spontaneously generated two beers, and second, that Darius would expect some form of compensation for his troubles. Not that he'd need money to buy the beer. She could count on him lifting it, and he would welcome the challenge that it had to be Schaefer, specifically. Her concern was rather that his interests in her welfare were not purely humanitarian. But as Arnold had never beaten her quite so severely as this, so that three days later she still found it impossible to lie on

her side without losing her breath to an electric shock of pain, the risks seemed manageable.

2) Hide the crown: During the last three beatings he'd worn it, and Lorna concluded that the worst beatings, the angriest ones, the ones with repeated blows, came when he was crowned. She had to hide it. "Why not destroy it?" you ask. Lorna had considered this. But what if she burned the crown, or threw it into the school garbage bin, and its disappearance catapulted Arnold into an unremitting rage? His crown could not be replaced, but it could be restored if hiding it backfired and they were blamed. She could furtively remove it to some place where he would find it.

But both strategies proved impossible. Lorna couldn't steal the crown. It never left Arnold's person, its brief stint by the garbage that one morning having been an aberration. Her opportunities came when Arnold fell asleep during *Magnum P.I.*, and they depended on his left hip pocket being exposed. Once she had steeled herself sufficiently to try picking his pocket, she began to appreciate the complexity of that art. The crown rarely peeked out. Lorna did manage once to dislodge it completely, but in a single, unwaking motion, Arnold retrieved it from the seat, shoved it into a front pocket, and rolled onto his opposite side. It was the closest she came to success.

As for keeping the beer supply flowing, Darius went missing again shortly after he caught Arnold beating Lorna.

He was gone for six months, his longest absence ever, and by the date of his return, the landscape had altered enough to make Lorna's reform strategies obsolete.

I refer to Chester's death. Arnold lost his temper as well as two weeks' pay at a new card game at the Sanitation warehouse, and now he was laying low. That, at least, is what Aunt Flo had heard, so Lorna and her brothers were again at Flo's overnight. They watched *Wheel of Fortune*, then *Jeopardy*, then a marathon of *Fresh Prince of Bel Air* repeats. They ate several boxes of Milk Duds. Chester said he felt sick and crawled off to bed in Darius' room. Everyone else fell asleep in front of the TV. The fire chief determined that the blaze started in a pile of magazines and trash next to the radiator in Darius' room. Chester had closed the door and probably died from smoke inhalation even before the alarm went off over Aunt Flo's recliner. Flo died from the smoke, too, her breathing already so compromised, although the fire department did arrive in time to get her out of the house. Lorna vaguely recalled the screeching smoke alarm, waking, dragging Buggy with her as she crawled toward the door and onto the front stoop. Buggy couldn't remember anything all. After a brief stay in the hospital, they were removed from Arnold's custody and, within a week, placed in foster care with Ms. Alice Clampitt-Bernstein, where they remained for two years.

Buggy and Lorna's time with Ms. Alice is the stuff of another story, but you should know something about how she affected Lorna and Buggy. Consider this much: she cooked hot breakfasts, she played *Sorry!* even when she had the flu, she never talked about money, she could explain the parts of a sentence. Buggy grew deeply attached to her, Lorna appreciated her but kept a distance, and then they were moved back to their father. Several months of therapy, a parenting course, and regular participation in Gambler's Anonymous made him no longer unfit to care for them, according to Judge Mitchell of Family Court.

Indeed, the years of violent physical abuse seemed to be over. Arnold was able to ignore Buggy's sadness and reticence after the children's removal from Ms. Alice, even if he was incapable of offering comfort. He never stopped at Sinja's or the pool hall, he never disappeared for weekends. The crown was gone. He'd taken up cigarettes, but everyone needs a habit, and he never smoked indoors. When he got angry, he went outside and counted aloud, no matter the weather or how many people were around. The heat was only turned off twice in Lorna's remaining years at home. There was usually enough food in the refrigerator. He had put a wallet-sized photograph of Chester, framed, on top of the TV, which he dusted regularly.

Reformation. Lorna could not claim to have engineered

it, but she was cautiously optimistic that it was permanent. You know otherwise, since you're already aware that there is an impending violent altercation between a teenage Buggy and his father. But suppose you did not know. Still you would have predicted Arnold's recidivism and Lorna's disappointment. Unlike Lorna, you've learned that it's best to be skeptical because that softens the blow. Lorna would say you're bruised all the same, so the question is whether you're hopelessly beaten, or beaten but hopeful.

There's nothing for it now but to tell you how Buggy killed Arnold. By the time that happened, several years after Chester's death and Arnold's reforms, Lorna had moved out on her own. She had become a medical assistant through the training program at Baptist Hospital and taken an apartment with Cindy Gonzalez, another nurse. Buggy didn't tell Lorna when Arnold began being away at nights again, and he said nothing when their father stopped counting when his temper flared. Arnold's outbursts seemed mild by comparison to the early years of abuse. He might shove Buggy or hurl the remote at him. Usually Buggy figured he had it coming, because he was sullen and impudent to his father. What's more, he believed that since he was now taller and heavier than Arnold, he could take him, if it came to that. Why tell Lorna? Why disappoint her? Hadn't she survived and moved on?

So Lorna was surprised when Officer Wisniewski came to her apartment and summoned her to the station to fetch Buggy. Wisniewski, a calm man, explained that he and his fellow officers on the scene had clearly determined that Buggy had acted in self defense. The chief detective would corroborate this, he explained, and they doubted that the coroner's report would reveal anything surprising. Now a judge might determine that Buggy would need help, but no one would call this Buggy's fault.

Lorna recognized Officer Wisniewski, though he gave no indication that he knew her. He was the boyfriend of Sharon, who had been her and Buggy's caseworker from the time of the fire until they returned to Arnold. They had met once at the ice cream parlor in the mall. Lorna later noticed that the detective wore a class ring from the same year and school as her father. In a small city like theirs, she thought, such coincidences must not be uncommon. Anonymity is impossible, and it pays to be discrete.

When Arnold had shoved Buggy that evening, harder than usual, and with a reference to his ingratitude, the locked box of the boy's soul broke open and demons of every color filled the room. An officer walking the beat heard the screams of several voices, each saying a name over and over: Chester, Aunt Flo, Mama, Miss Alice. He radioed for backup, approached the front door, and looked through the window. Buggy was tearing around the apartment, emitting all those voices and destroying things. Arnold seemed to be mesmerized, transfixed in the center of the living room, his hands covering his head. The officer decided that the boy could be a danger to himself or others and entered the scene. Arnold snapped to and lunged toward the door just as Buggy whirled a floor lamp with the full force of his body. The lamp's base squared Arnold's left temple and the right side of his face smashed into the TV screen, toppling Chester's photo. No one noticed the picture until the detective arrived and found it saturated in blood from Arnold's head.

Lorna donated her father's body to the hospital, and his organs were harvested. She kept his rings. They are in her jewelry box. Chester's photo was ruined, so she threw it out.

Buggy, now 25 years old, has never beaten his children, though he sometimes hits his wife. He is careful not to hit her where the bruises will show, but she is less cautious when she strikes back.

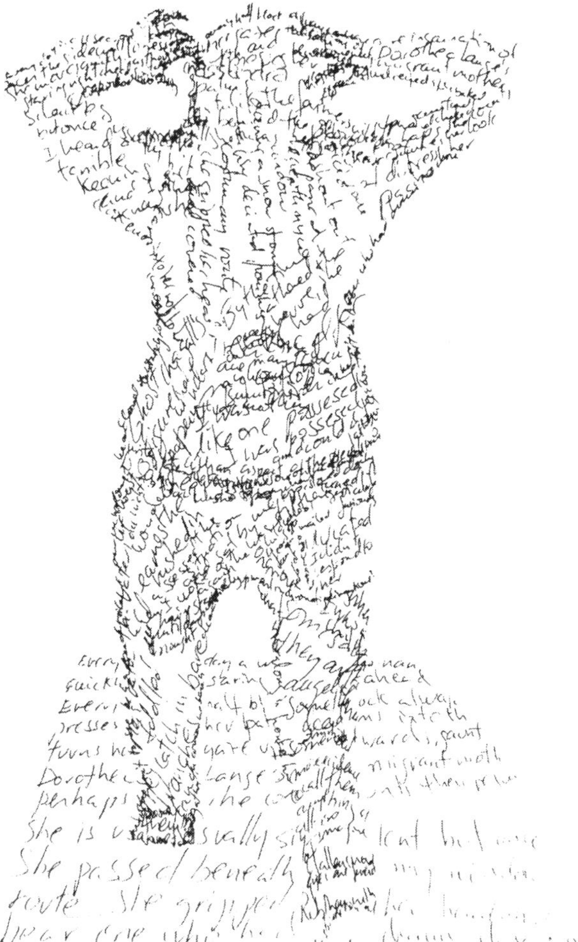

Dorothea Lange's
like one
She passed beneath

We Need Donors

It's true I hardly feel the needle, I keep my head turned and, trusting the nurse's question, describe my favorite game to her, but the very idea of blood leaving me seeps and spreads quickly, as water will overtake the surface through a crack in the ice, and I break through while she calls my name, though there's nothing to be done to stop my going under all those reds, the steady flow, the quotidian loss we've all come to expect, the soiled violet blotches on the highway, the polka dot on a band-aid, the liters siphoned from a corpse, the pools forming on the field where we are running and I grab the playground ball, hurl it at her, a welt forming on her bare leg as she hobbles back to home plate, out.

Little Boy Giving

As always, having something in hand—bottle caps he's found, a hockey puck, Charles (his stuffed penguin)—held firmly enough to prevent loss (but never grasped, for that is the difference between care and greed), he says "Look," placing it in his mother's hand, and "Keep it," not because giving brings gifts (although it often does to one who finds the perfect shard of blue glass and gives it up gladly) but because giving it to her is just as satisfying as having it for himself (the difference between him and her being a matter merely of space, which he easily wills away).

Coping Strategies

When they found Darius between the dumpsters behind Sinja's Deli, the syringe had grown into his skin, and his arm had turned black from the elbow down. He lost the arm and nearly his life. It took that much to finally break his habit—that, rehabilitation, and finding Jesus.

"That and finding Jesus." I'm not a preacher. Most of the time I'm not even a believer. This is not a tract. Please don't shut the door in my face.

Still, I say that Darius did sort of come back from the dead.

Janine had as much to do with his resurrection as Jesus or the Holy Ghost. Darius went to the Razor's Edge because he couldn't manage his clippers with one hand without leaving gaps in his buzz cut. Janine was his stylist for the day. She was a heavy-set girl, cheerful, with strawberry highlights in her frosted hair. Silence made her uncomfortable. To keep the conversation moving while she worked, she volunteered elaborate answers to her own questions. When Darius said, "I'm unemployed at the moment" to her "What do you do?", she described the fourteen months that she had been without a job after high school. "Honey, I just got so depressed being around the house, you know. Do you get that way? I sure do. I need to be doing. Well it just got worse and worse so as I couldn't even look for jobs no more, and my girlfriends got fed up with me 'cause I weren't even helping around the apartment, which I had been before to make up for not paying my share of the rent. They'd been so sweet, letting me get by with just cooking and doing laundry, being sort of like the house mama for the four of us, but who can blame them for getting fed up and saying, 'Janine, honey, you got to pull yourself together or we can't have you here no more.' I mean it was tough love and all, but it worked because that's what helped me decide to try doing hair. I always liked doing hair, and, well, one thing led to another, and here I am, fulfilled."

Next she told him about her trip to Ryman Auditorium, the "Mother Church of Country Music," in response to her own question about whether he liked the song playing on the salon radio. And after apologizing for potentially offending him by referring to Ryman as a church, she went on to describe Open Door Pentecostal, her actual church. "Lots of good, loving people there," she said as she turned Darius toward the mirror. "Now you did say 'high and tight,' right? I hope so, 'cause that is sure enough what I've done!"

The date that sealed it for Darius and Janine was the Singles With Holy Spirit trip to the Powhatan Pier for the Easter Sunrise service. God outdid himself, the group leader said, and it's true that the sky and ocean were a swirl of violet and rose for the duration of "Because He Lives, I Can Face Tomorrow." Darius was troubled in his heart and asked the leader to join him and Janine in private because he needed to make a confession. They broke away from the group, and by the bait tank at the pier's end Darius told the truth about his missing arm. It hadn't been crushed in a car accident as he'd claimed when Janine asked him about it on their first date. He had been a junkie, he explained, and lost control entirely after his mother, Flo, died in a house fire while he was out using. In hindsight he figured he was trying to kill himself with heroin, and he'd come damn close to being success-ful. But he was clean now, he had been for thirteen months, Praise Jesus, and he believed that God must have a reason for sparing him. He just didn't know what it was.

Weeping, Janine exclaimed, "To be my husband and Daddy to my future children!" The group leader blushed and stood speechless. But since he was an ordained Pentecostal minister, he agreed to marry them at sunset on the pier if they'd hurry and get a license.

Janine soon learned that about once per week, Darius

was startled awake at night by jolts of electricity shooting up his missing arm and into his shoulder. Someone flicking a breaker on and off, that's what it felt like, and he could not make it stop. The first time it happened after their marriage, Janine phoned Starr, her girlfriend, who was an RN at the Baptist hospital, and she diagnosed it as phantom pain. "A doctor probably can't do much about it," Starr explained, "but maybe a psychiatrist could give him some coping strategies."

Meaning no disrespect to Starr, who was a kind friend, Darius explained to Janine that with nearly two years now of rehab and recovery to draw on, he hoped he knew as much as any shrink about coping strategies. Darius was now custodian at the YMCA, and, as he put it, "Baby, a janitor can't afford mental health care any more than a hairdresser." He would come up with a way to deal with his phantom.

That's how Darius and Janine started their midnight walks around Spring Garden, the development where they'd rented a duplex. For months, Janine wouldn't allow him to go alone. She was afraid that when he was in so much pain, he might be tempted to use. She felt almost unfaithful, doubting him like this. She never admitted it to him, and he didn't suspect it. He took her at her word: she came because she couldn't stand him being in pain by himself. It wasn't untrue, just not the whole truth.

Janine wasn't splitting hairs. I'm not splitting them for her. She would have gone to share the pain even if she'd had no idea he was in recovery. But his history gave it a sense of urgency.

And maybe Darius did suspect her of not entirely, one-hundred-percent trusting he couldn't get through this without at least being tempted to relapse. If so, he might have thought, "Who can blame her?", which is what I would have thought, too. It's one of the ways that Darius and I are alike, the difference being he'd never make you listen to his story, whereas I think you need to hear it.

2

Although Lisa had not been thrilled when her mother began dating the manager of Spring Garden, it had bene-fits. Lisa had been allowed to have a key to the roof access above their apartment. After reading about container gardening, she built a set of boxes from scrap lumber and filled them with peat and potting soil. She had gotten most of her materials from the gardener's shed for the development. All she had to purchase with her cat-sitting and dog-walking money were seeds and seedlings. Tomatoes (she preferred heirloom varieties,) lettuce (Romaine and arugula), cabbage, yellow squash, carrots, snap peas, broccoli, and red pota-toes. Vegetables only. Flowers did not interest her. In the early fall, she would try mustard and yams. For all this, she could tolerate her mother's romance.

Lisa devised ways to avoid what bothered her about the manager and her mother. At night she often sat in her garden to escape the noises from her mother's bedroom. Her mother was silent, but the manager was an enormous man who seemed to require a lot of oxygen to perform his tasks. These didn't bear thinking about, but you can't turn off your imagination. In June the evenings were mild, and except that waking up at 6:30 to walk Mrs. Tucker's Labrador was hard after a late night, Lisa didn't mind being on the roof. She had a lounge chair and a reading light that clamped to her book. It was comfortable. If she sometimes feared that her life was becoming a wannabe *Secret Garden*, she countered that she had no affinity for robins or sickly cousins.

She couldn't dislike the manager, and if he wanted to try hard to win her over, she wouldn't dissuade him by being sour or resentful. Tonight, he had brought over Chinese food. He remembered that she'd ordered bean curd and broccoli once when the three of them had gone out, so he'd gotten some, although neither he nor her mother cared for it. He was attentive in that way. He asked about her garden, specific things, like "how are your Cherokee purples faring" and "are your plants getting enough action from the bees?" True, some of this seemed calculated. She was annoyed by how confidently he bestowed his gifts and indulgences. But maybe she wasn't being fair. Maybe she should appreciate that he was trying for her. Arlene's mother had a boyfriend who came over, got drunk, and slapped her butt when her mom wasn't looking. By comparison, she shouldn't complain, the manager's nightly huffing and puffing aside. Her mother seemed to enjoy his companionship and hadn't changed in order to please him. Not the way middle-aged women did in movies. She didn't mewl and fawn, she hadn't bought a lace teddy. She just got into her pajamas, as always, and she and the manager went into her bedroom together. Tonight, in fact, he'd gone in first and fallen asleep, and Lisa guessed nothing was going to happen. But the breathing started around 2AM, just as she'd told Arlene that she had to sign off.

So here she was, in her lounge chair among her vegetable plants. There was a full moon, and its reflection off the white asphalt roofing made everything glow. A spider had built a web between her tomato stakes. Up close the web's wrinkled sheets proved to be an involuted weave of layers. Only the most aerobatic midge could have navigated through the tiny unaligned gaps. What would it be like to fly into that, Lisa wondered? If you were that small, the web would be a massive cage, swaying between skyscraper pinnacles high above the earth's surface. Maybe it was somehow hidden in plain sight so that you were destined to smash into it just as it came fully into view. Your struggle just made more bars collapse and twist around you. Nothing to do but wait to be eaten.

As it was, she could destroy the cage easily. She could do it with a single swipe of her hand. Not that she ever would. Anyway, wouldn't the spider just rebuild? She looked around for him. Tiny and red, he was perched on a closed tomato flower. Yes, almost immediately, he would re-weave the entire edifice. Light skated along the threads. Lisa could pinch him between her fingers right there on the yellow flower's pursed lips. But why would such a thought come into her head? She would be even less apt to crush the spider than to obliterate his web.

There were whispers from the parking lot below. Lisa held her breath and listened. Although it was always quiet on the roof, she couldn't make out sentences, just tones and occasional words. One was a woman's voice, speaking the way a nurse does when the doctor is giving you a shot. Lisa peered over. The woman was large, wearing a crimson kimono, and she was stroking the bald head of a one-armed man. Something appeared to be wrong with him besides the missing arm. They would walk along slowly, then he would gasp and draw up, as if he'd jumped into an icy pool, and his girlfriend would embrace him. Lisa thought she heard, "I love you. It's okay." She couldn't be sure, but that's what should be said under the circumstances.

And what were the circumstances? Maybe he had cancer. An arm had to be amputated, and his hair was lost to radiation. So sad. They were both young, maybe even newlyweds. Already there was drama in their lives. Wasn't that always the case in marriages? One gets sick or hurt or depressed and the other becomes his nurse. Either that or one gets tired of the other, as her father had when she was still in diapers, and just runs off to something new.

Lisa pulled back. Had she invaded their privacy? She tried to shut out the whispers, but now that they were so close, it was as if the couple were right there in the garden with her. The man kept repeating, "It has to stop, it has to stop," and his wife, "It will, I love you, it will, I love you." Lisa crept further back and accidentally bumped a tomato stake. She glanced over her shoulder. The vast net shimmered under the moon. The spider waited.

3

As he walked from Anita's apartment to his office, Drew thought again about marriage. Anita was expecting him to ask. Maybe Lisa was, too. He had not set out to become so involved, but things had progressed. It was possible to describe matters now as love. He had no objection to that. Perhaps he even felt it. Marriage tended to follow.

Anita had not put pressure on him. On the contrary, she

was so scarred by her ex-husband that she had insisted on proceeding with caution around every bend: flirtation, the first date, the kiss (yes, even the kiss), the sex (a milestone), and now essentially cohabiting. From his perspective, after months of cautious maneuvering, he had created the ideal situation for everyone. He was welcomed, she was relaxed and indulgent.

Drew pulled the shades and turned on his computer. The chimes and the whir, the sputtering of Mr. Coffee in the lobby, the zing of the weedeaters trimming the curb outside his window: why add wedding bells? That was cold, he thought, but he was satisfied with their lives. He hesitated to change anything, and he wondered whether Anita would understand if he explained it that way. "We've outgrown marriage," he would explain. "We can keep on this way, enjoying and supporting each other without it."

The front door buzzed as someone entered. From the chair behind his desk, he could see her, one of his tenants, Janine. He was good with names. Had to be in his line of work. Janine fumbled with her hair. The secretary was away at the dentist. There was no one to direct her.

Drew called out cheerfully, "How can I help you this morning, Miss Janine?" and rolled himself into view.

"Oh, good morning, Mr. Wisniewski. I won't take much of your time. I was just on my way to work and thought I'd stop and get an update on that shower rail."

"Sure, sure. Let me check on that. Get yourself coffee." Drew punched a few keys on his computer. Janine fiddled with the small golden cross on her charm bracelet. "Order should arrive tomorrow, and I'll put my men right on it."

Janine walked over and put her hand out to shake. Drew took it. "Okay. Thank you, sir. I'm not trying to be pushy. It's just that Darius slipped again. He'd flip out if he knew I was asking for this, but once it's installed, we'll *all* be better for it." Janine did her best to affect a knowing stare.

Drew sat back down and looked at his computer screen. "Of course. Like I say, I'll put my men right on it."

The weedeaters swarmed loudly, drowning out the door buzzer as Janine left. Drew had not put in the work order the first time that Janine requested it, even though installing the rail would probably serve to protect him as well as Darius. He had been trying to find a reason to terminate Janine's lease once he realized who Darius was. Drew had heard plenty about Darius. He knew the kind. Drew's brother Jackson had been the officer on call when Darius' mother died in the house fire a while back. A kid had died, too. No relation—the mother was babysitting—but where was Darius during all this? Strung out on heroin. It took the detectives almost a week to track him down to claim his mother's body. Then he went on a bender, and it was Jackson's partner who put him in the ambulance with a syringe scabbed over in his gangrenous arm. Said it stood out stiff as a pecker. That was two years ago. Supposedly Darius was clean. But Drew couldn't be sure. He knew this much about people: if you're a junkie, you're a junkie. They couldn't cut that off like his rotted arm.

I can say this much in Drew's defense: he's right that we don't stop being addicts. Everyone who's read *People* magazine or watched a cop show knows that much, right? "Hello, I'm your narrator, and I'm a recovering addict." It's a marker, a trait. I'm not asking you to ignore who Darius is, anymore than I'd have you ignore me. Drew just tended to see a recovering junkie and a user as essentially the same and nothing more.

Drew did get the handrail installed. He didn't need a tenant cracking his head in the shower and supplementing his disability checks with damages awarded from a lawsuit.

4

Lisa went out on the roof again the next night. She didn't go to escape the manager's noises. He was in their apartment, as usual, but her mother's room was quiet. She went to be in her garden.

She watched the red spider reinforce his web and wait. The air was still tonight and so quiet that she felt she could hear his shuffle along his wire. Actually, that sound came from the pavement below. She expected to see the couple when she looked over the ledge, but it was the woman by herself, her slippers scrapping along. As if on cue, she glanced up and saw Lisa, who seemed to be in a spotlight of the moon.

"Honey, what are you doing up there? Why are you on the roof, and at night, too? Are you by yourself?" Janine studied Lisa's face: freckled and plain, a bit sad. Her hair was oily and pulled back in a barrette. She had a row of piercings in her right ear and a small ring in her nose.

"I'm sitting in my garden. I have a garden up here."

"Well I'll be. On the roof? There's dirt up there? Well I'll be."

"Would you like to see it?"

"Well of course, honey. I've seen roof gardens in pictures of New York City, but never down here. Do I need to climb a ladder?"

"No, stay put. I'll show you the way up."

When she opened the roof door to usher Janine in, Lisa was suddenly embarrassed. She had never considered how ragged her garden boxes looked or how few plants she had altogether. Her garden was tidy—you could say that for it— but desperate. She feared that Janine was going to ask if she had done this by herself. That was how people responded to pitiful, earnest displays, like what you say when a four-year-old draws you a picture. Lisa prevented it.

"It's a far cry from the Hanging Gardens of Babylon."

Janine cinched the belt of her kimono. "Well I don't know nothing about that, but I'm just impressed. Impressed! Honey, you must have a green thumb. I tried to grow a tomato once and it was the pitifullest sight you ever saw, pale and wilty and not one single tomato. No ma'am, God did not mean for me to be a farmer so thank goodness I was born where there's supermarkets. But you—well this is unique, truly unique. I don't believe you told me your name, honey."

Janine and Lisa talked for over an hour. Lisa said far more than she meant to. She went on for too long about heirloom tomatoes and natural pest control. She mentioned the manager and that she didn't like the way men sounded when they did it. She circled back to her garden, what she hoped to plant in the fall and maybe expand into next year. Germinating her own seeds, for example. Janine talked even more than Lisa, but she didn't say as much, just things that made Lisa feel at ease. She would tell you that that comes of being a hairdresser.

She did explain why she was out walking. Her sweet husband suffered from phantom pain in his missing arm, but tonight he had fallen sound asleep as soon as he hit the bed, and she was afraid that she would wake him up with all her restlessness, so she went out by herself. Lisa was secretly grateful to have some of the couple's mystery clarified. Surely phantom pain was preferable to cancer.

Janine realized that she should get back home in case Darius woke up. "Honey, I have so enjoyed this," she declared. "I know you're probably not the styling salon type, but you do have to drop by and see me at Razor's Edge. Just to visit. It's kind of my version of your garden, you understand? And if you feel a little daring, I can put some red highlights in your hair that would pick up the gold flecks in your eyes. Free of charge, of course."

Lisa never went, although she considered it from time to time, and whenever they saw each other, she and Janine waved as if they were friends.

5

It took another two months for the manager to build up his resolve and make his case to Anita. We've outgrown marriage, things are steady and pleasant, why risk change. Unsurprised and unhappy, Anita refused to see him any longer. He took away Lisa's key to the roof.

This was in late August, right before school started. He claimed that he wasn't being vindictive, that if he was no longer family, he couldn't risk the liability of Lisa doing something against company policy. Anita retorted that he had never been family, because family demands the commitment expressed by marriage, and he was too selfish to commit. He disagreed, of course, and he was sorry that she couldn't see the reason in his point of view. In any case, he didn't want to be the cause of Lisa's gardening coming to an end. He would allow her to move her containers to the small patch of grass in front of their buildings. She could have the help of his staff. But Lisa didn't want a consolation gift for her mother's break-up. It made the garden seem desperate. And beside the imitation nature of Spring Garden's curbs— the manicured beds of impatiens, the miniature Japanese maples, the pungent cedar mulch—her plants would be an eyesore until the deer ate them up.

So her remaining tomatoes, squash, arugula...everything withered on the roof. Sometimes at night Lisa imagined the plants above her, dried and crumbling. This became part of a dream she had throughout high school. She sat in a parched garden, and either she was very small or the plants were tremendous, because she was under a canopy of browning vines and leaves. She was thirsty, so much so that her tongue was hardening, and although she knew there was a watering can, she couldn't remember where.

Sometimes she thought of going to the Razor's Edge and telling Janine about the dream. Janine would have welcomed her, listened and babbled with the delightful, soothing profusion of a spring falls. But Lisa didn't want to be soothed, and she didn't want to trivialize her sorrow by hearing that it would pass. Soon it would begin to spin a web around her heart. Why would she let someone brush it away?

6

Darius started this story of common sorrows, and now, near the end, is when I confess that I loved Darius. Especially when he was a junkie, I loved him, because he had wit enough to see his flaws, if not enough discipline to do anything about them before he hit bottom. He was funnier then, and he was daring. You may be inclined to doubt that Darius can hold what's left of himself together. I *could* say, "I knew him when…", wink and nod, hedging my bets so that if you come to me next year and declare, "He's off the wagon" or "He's still on it," either way I prove to be wise. It's tempting to do that, but it's cowardly. I'll at least be bold enough to predict that Darius will survive everyone in this narrative, including me.

Darius became addicted to his evening walks. By his own account, "addicted" is not an exaggeration. Whether in pain or not, at midnight he grew agitated, felt hollow, eerily similar to the sensation of needing a fix. Janine learned not to try to persuade him to stay inside, because if he did so, it was only to please her, and his subsequent irritability was not worth her triumph. He loved her company but would insist that she not feel obliged to traipse out with him, especially when the weather turned.

So he was alone on the November evening that he saw Lisa by the Spring Garden dumpsters. There was a cold, steady rain. The trouble lights on the building eves were splotches of wet yellow, but the one near the dumpsters dripped just enough to highlight the girl. Janine had pointed her out to Darius once, and he knew the story of their nighttime encounter. They'd never met, but he was easy enough to recognize. Lisa was staring at a heap of lumber, twine, and broken tomato stakes. Darius didn't want to startle her, so he splashed loudly along the pavement as he approached.

Lisa turned. She was in flannel pajamas, soaked, her hair matted to her thin face, a water bead depending from her nose ring. She pushed her hair from her eyes and crossed her arms over her chest.

"Don't you need a jacket or something?" Darius asked.

"I'm okay, thanks," Lisa mumbled.

"I would offer you mine, but it seems pointless now you're sopping wet. Why'd you come out in your pajamas?"

"I don't know. I mean, I wasn't too concerned about getting wet." She was shaking.

"What else is there to be concerned about if you're going out in the rain?"

Lisa shrugged. Darius gestured at the pile. "Are those what's left of your garden? If you want to salvage any of it, I can help."

"I saw it from my bedroom window," Lisa said. "The maintenance men must have finally torn it down."

The rain became heavier. Lisa pushed her hair away from her eyes. She imagined Darius and Janine on their evening walks, talking about the girl with the roof garden and sometimes looking up to catch a glimpse of her. Had they realized she was never there after the summer? Maybe Janine had called up to her and had been disappointed not to hear a reply.

Darius lifted a board from the pile. "It's a dang waste for them to throw all this out. This one could be re-used." He began sorting the boards, sighting down them as if he were a carpenter and it weren't too dark to see the flaws. "There's a community garden over by the Pentecostal church. Janine's always wanting to try a garden, but she's bad luck to plants. If I stored this stuff till spring, maybe you could help her get it right."

Lisa could see where this was headed, the pity of it, and the kindness. She wanted to refuse, and she didn't want to refuse. Saying nothing, she helped gather boards and stakes and carry them to Darius' door. It was a long time before spring.

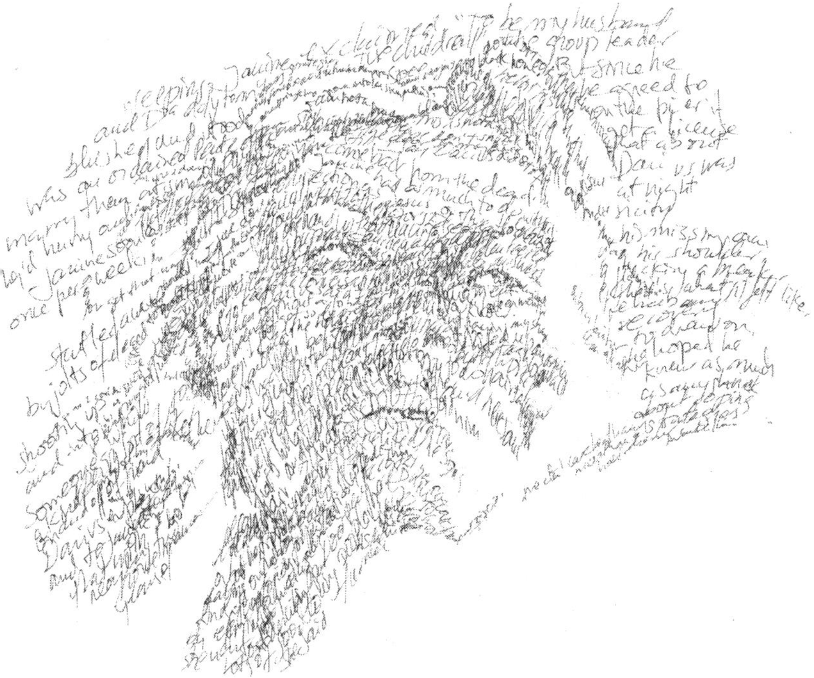

Sighs too deep for tears

(December 14, 2012)

As I rock and feed the baby, Elizabeth, I read her a Christina Rossetti poem from a book of nursery rhymes:

Under the ivy bush
One sits sighing,
And under the willow tree
One sits crying:--

Under the ivy bush
Cease from your sighing,
But under the willow tree
Lie down a-dying.

Elizabeth sighs, not longingly as in the somber lyric, but with contentment. She drifts off. I put down the nursery rhymes but can't reach my novel. Sigh. If I call to my teenage son to fetch it, because I dare not move and wake the baby, he will sigh in exasperation, having to pause the video on his tiny hand-held screen. Elizabeth sighs in fullness, Jacob in frustration, and I out of lack. Whatever our moods, all this long exhaling suggests that at least there is enough breath, even more than enough, for sustenance.

I rock quietly and listen. The radio is turned down low. Through the fading signal, Mahler's *Kindertotenlieder*. "Ein Lämplein verlosch in meinem Zelt," the soprano sighs. A little lamp goes out in my tent.

I could be mishearing. Something is not quite right. With "sighs too deep for tears," I once said, misquoting Wordsworth, and the professor gasped. A gasp is a sigh in reverse, the quick inhalation, a sign of shock or surprise (not of the mild variety). "I believe you mean, 'Thoughts that do often lie too deep for tears'?" he asked breathlessly. The sigh too deep for tears would be an unfathomable melancholy, a bottomless Werther-like sorrow. And yet its very profundity signifies feeling. We have not exhausted the sentiments, it says. We are not numb to the suffering of others. Such sighing has had diverse, noble practitioners: Hamlet over Yorick, Virginia Woolf at the brink of the pond, President Lincoln after Gettysburg. The heavy breath hollows us out, helpless, confirmed in our pessimism.

The music has stopped abruptly, but the volume is too soft for me to make out all the announcer's words. She seems panicked. She seems to be weeping. "At an elementary school in Newtown, Connecticut." Elizabeth sighs again as she sinks deeper into rest. Ein Lämplein verlosch. I get still. I strain to hear the news.

Then I strain to keep it out. Under the willow tree, lie down a-dying. I have been accused of sighing too much, and rarely out of contentedness. It's a fair criticism. Who has not used the sigh as a passive-aggressive tactic? A cowardly maneuver, because coming right out and saying what is wrong would prove the pettiness of my discontent. "Keep that up, young man," a father warns, "and I'll give you something to sigh about." On most days, we clean and well-fed people have few problems that warrant the ashen sorrow in which I sit, sighing for a bare bodkin.

On some day, Jane Kenyon remarks, it will be otherwise. Now there is weeping in the breathy signal of the radio. Do they know how many, she asks. There are still several unaccounted for, he replies. Oft denk' ich, sie sind nur ausgegangen. Maybe they've just gone out. Maybe they're hidden in a cabinet or pretending to be dead. I try not to hear any more. Mark but this baby in her contentment. Meditate and be cheerful. Besides, did not medieval philosophers teach that with each sigh, your lifespan was reduced, since we only have so many breaths allotted to us? Or maybe I'm conflating the doctrines of the humors and predestination. The news fades in and out like breathing. Sighs too deep for tears. Deep in his video game next door, Jacob perishes. He sighs.

One who sighs is prone to look behind or beyond, to be always reflecting or anticipating. I imagine that the Buddha learned not to sigh in becoming aware of his breath. Jesus, on the other hand, began and ended as a sigher: at Mary's breast by the manger, contented despite the cold makeshift accommodations; and on the cross, after sipping vinegar and protesting that his father had abandoned him.

There is the weeping again, through the static, just above the threshold of my rocking chair's creaking. Elizabeth stirs slightly. She will not want to be put down. Our babies never did. As an infant, my oldest son, Samuel, would gasp as I laid him down. Slowly I would back away from the crib and turn off the little lamp—the magic lantern that spun slowly and cast the colored shadows of a carousel. Ein Lämplein verlosch. We drop them off at school. They learn to trot off happily. We watch until they disappear.

Under the ivy bush, one sat sighing. "Stop sighing!" his father demanded, so he retreated up his favorite tree and wedged himself in a crook. Ivy had nearly overtaken the trunk and dangled from the branches like tassels. He would have been invisible but for his sighing. All that heavy, humid breath among the leaves was a localized weather front, a tiny cyclone. Did the branch toss with his windy sighs, or was he so preoccupied by the troubles that occasioned his sighing that he lost his balance? Either way, he tipped backward from his perch. Gasp! Imagine that word colored red, in bold comic sans lettering, snapping like a banner above his head against the deceptively verdant backdrop of the canopy. Our young hero grasped for the tail of the speech bubble. It snapped off in his hand like a skink's appendage, wriggled and disappeared, and his fall resumed. But fortune favored him. The long pogo of the "p" in "gasp" slid through the bubble's aperture, our hero grabbed it, and he drifted downward as if he held a balloon. Feet firmly on the ground, he sighed in relief.

I sing to drown out the sorrow on the radio. "When the bough breaks, the cradle will fall." Most of the time, Samuel would startle awake if we tried to lay him in his crib. Having found a correlation between crib death and sleeping on the belly, medical science enjoined us young parents to put our infants down on their backs. But infants retain an ancient memory of falling that manifests in a dramatic startle reflex: a gasp and a flailing outward of the arms. For Samuel, however deep in sleep he seemed, tipping backward into the crib must have stirred up primordial nightmares—Lucifer hurling over the walls of paradise, or a helpless simian slipping from his mother's arms high in the treetops. The gasp, the flail: in the beginning, my wife and I were filled with parental empathy, but in time Samuel's startle reflex became our enemy, casting aspersions on our fitness as parents, keeping all of us awake. We solved the problem by nestling Samuel down in his infant car seat, the detachable kind that stayed in his room except when we were driving. Putting Sammy to bed involved slowly sliding him from a cradled position in my arms into the tiny chair, which kept his arms snug against his sides. Even still there could be the gasp, but without the flail it transformed into a yawn. Soon followed a sigh. I would then lift the car seat into Sammy's crib—a purely cosmetic step, I suppose, that made him seem to be fully tucked in.

The radio sighs static and anger and tears. Elizabeth breathes slowly. It's grey outside. Ein Lämplein verlosch in meinem Zelt. The trees are bare. The swings are empty. Oft denk' ich, sie sind nur ausgegangen. I often think they have just gone out, soon to return. Rock-a-bye baby, in the treetop. "Who puts her baby in a tree?" Jacob once asked incredulously. With the assistance of Wikipedia, I propose the following answers: (1) American Indian women of the 17th century, who made birchbark cradles and suspended them from branches; (2) The much-despised English Catholics, because the baby is thought to represent the papist heir to James II, and the wind that upsets the cradle is triumphant Protestantism; (3) A doting father, who dandles his youngster from his arm, imitating the way a branch suspends a swing.

Mother gasps, "Don't dandle him like that! What if you drop him? What if he hits his head? Then where will we be?" Father sighs and sets the child down.

The branches wave. When the bough breaks, the cradle will fall. Elizabeth has settled again. I cannot be in this rocker with her forever. Every cradle is balanced on a thin branch, under stress, the wind rising. We put our babies there because we must. Moses in the bulrushes, Jesus in the cattle trough: we make do, and the conditions are always precarious. That baby's sigh of contentment sounds no different from the sigh of disappointment it will become. I have to put her down, on her back, knowing she'll gasp. Why have you forsaken me?

Next door Jacob gasps at the events on his tiny screen. Now he knows, too. The radio crackles like gunfire. A little lamp goes out in my tent. Under the willow tree, one sits crying. Sigh for him, with thoughts that lie too deep for tears.

Evensong

Aubade III

A cluster of kinglets
Hidden ruby crowns,

Dim morning light
Brightened surfaces
Cormorant's shaded crest,

A green heron presses
Slowly through the cattails,
Rare, in October.

A young buck, one spike gone,
Lopsided unicorn, sips.

Vascar Retires

When age had finally overcome good sense, Vascar would strip naked on frosty mornings, take a bar of Ivory soap and his hat, dash down the hill like a child to a school bus and bathe in the icy pond, singing "In the sweet by and by" loud enough to make God wince. He would turn up in the most unlikely places and knock off at the most unlikely times: we found him napping at mid-morning in the middle of our dirt road, he sat an entire Thursday on our porch watching the black Angus bull kneel and chew, he chatted with people we could not see about nothing in particular.

Sometime between seventy and eighty he had kicked off his steel-toed shoes, thrown out or (better) just left behind the hammer, the ruler, the account book with which he had made a life like the barns he raised, stable and weatherproof, carefully planned that no space was wasted.

Now light-headed and limber he bobbed along like a cork on a line, bound to us but floating, and we dared not take our eyes off him. Think of what we would have missed!

Why, in his final hours the ulcer in his stomach spat rubies when he laughed, and the dirt in his hands grew muscadine vines and morning glory.

Portrait of John

Cornucopia

Dozens of cans filled the barn, Maxwell House, King's Syrup, Prince Albert, artifactual evidence of brand loyalty, yes, but also of his economy, these having contained the few daily rations (one might call them indulgences) he could not himself grow or make, and now having been given a second purpose, well within their scope, to hold screws, bolts, nails, washers, hardware of the widest variety, found, saved, donated, such that in gray, sodden November, the cold beginning of the fallow season between harvest and the next planting, he might with persistent rummaging find the very pieces needed to repair broken implements, repair and preparation being the purpose of winter, especially given so many cans, his ingenuity, and time, the second life of most things, and that only a fool discards without regret.

Ahab

Pain was fully known to him, its amplitude, its frequencies, the diverse shapes and complex spectrum of its waves, the specificity and elusiveness—his missing arm, for example, that itched inside and froze under blankets—the kind of torment that in fact defies calculation and precise description even though we resort to numbers, as when he was dying of cancer and his doctor would ask, "on a scale of one to ten, with ten being almost unbearable," the "almost" a sign of the infinite decimal places before ten, an infernal number whose flames would sear the cornea and yet turning from his doctor he would set his jaw and stare it down.

Westerns

He preferred *Gunsmoke* to *The Wild Wild West*, the Winchester to gadgetry and self-consciousness, and yet John Wayne over Clint Eastwood, the incandescent artifice of Romance over realism, which he once dismissed as "fiction," when I was home sick—"puny," he would say—from school and stretched out on the couch in his tiny living room, the stove groaning as he wedged another log into the firebox, the television a nuisance to him because there were only game shows at this time of day, and I was reading *The Grapes of Wrath*, about which he allowed, "I ain't got time for fiction about what I've lived," which was not to say truth is stranger than fiction, but that the truth of fiction was dust in his mouth and oil stains in the whorls of his one remaining hand.

Stumbling Block

His wicked laugh, loud and sharp, indulgent to the point of breathlessness, spattered with the sputum of a smoker's coughs, ricocheted around the room, polytonal in its wickedness—the B-movie villain's laugh, the full-bellied delight of the Ghost of Christmas Present, the school boy anticipating a dirty joke—such that I in my tortured asceticism would call forward images of direst cruelty and suffering to suppress my laughter but most often would fail, despite what I knew to be the consequences, not just for my soul but his (for woe unto him who causes a stumbling block), so together we chuckled down the primrose way to the everlasting bonfire.

Pneumonia Weather

The old people called it "pneumonia weather," because it lured you outdoors underdressed in January and slipped into your lungs the way field mice sneak into the pantry after the ground freezes. You don't notice them until the cornmeal is ruined with their droppings. The young are especially susceptible to mice as well as pneumonia weather, because they won't read the signs and take precautions. Plug the holes in the baseboards. Never go out in short sleeves or hatless before March, and if you're foolish enough to do so, take the subsequent cough seriously. By the time winter came back, recommitting us to the austerity of closed windows and covered skin, Reverend Moody had preached six funerals, none for a body over thirty years old. The Kilpatricks' baby disturbed me most, but Mother disagreed. "Everyone trembles at the death of a baby," she commiserated, "but the greater tragedy is Nora Hopkins." Nora's children were nine and eleven, too young to cope with such grief but old enough to feel it thoroughly. I suppose Mother was right. But the baby's white coffin floated through my room at nights. There was a lamb carved in its lid. When I closed my eyes or when I tried to stop thinking, it surfaced like a bobber to remind me that there's nothing holding us here that can't let go.

Winter in the southern foothills comes in sudden, disrespectful outbursts. It is a full-handed slap across the cheek. Days of tepid rain give way to a warm snap, but then temperatures plummet and the world is ice fog and frozen mud. At least in New England, where I lived briefly as a student, there is the picturesque relief of snowfall. Around home, there is only sleet and freezing rain and misery. Mercifully, winter is brief. Not long after the last yard ornament Nativity scene has been boxed up, crocuses appear. When sleet returns to smack them down, Mother says the pagan Greeks were right: the Fates are capricious and the gods vengeful. "We Baptists, with our blessed assurances of the resurrection, could learn a thing or two from Sophocles," she would explain.

Mother was an autodidact. She read continuously, and had she been born into a house with a library and educated parents, she might have become a Nietzsche scholar or a member of the Historical Jesus seminar. But the gods delight in our struggles—at least so Mother always said—and watching a brilliant child languish in an intellectual desert was pure Schadenfreude. For her liberal arts education, she relied on Funk & Wagnall's—a set purchased with bonus stamps from the supermarket in Lewisburg—and the eclectic shelves of the bookmobile. That Bodleian on wheels was her salvation, and she never missed its two-hour stop over in the cemetery parking lot. Throughout my entire childhood, no matter anyone's poor health, no matter the weather, we sat in the lot once every three weeks and waited for the bookmobile to arrive.

On the day of Nora Hopkins' burial, we walked from the graveside to the bookmobile, which dared not leave before Mother paid her visit. A slow rain was beginning to freeze on the power lines and naked tree limbs, so when we climbed the steps of the converted school bus, Wilhelmina Greene sighed with relief. After us, she could leave in good conscience, since the threatening conditions surely warranted an early departure so long as Mother had been served. Miss Greene had honed her librarian's skills and increased her cultural literacy by learning to recommend titles based on Mother's reading habits. That day the stack included a handbook for grafting apple trees, an anthology of Jacobean drama, *The Sickness Unto Death*, and a book of Moravian recipes.

"Miss Mina, I am truly grateful that you came despite the weather, and I am so excited about the grafting handbook. What put that brilliant idea into your head?"

Mother knew it was her spate of animal husbandry

reading from the summer. Breeding miniature goats. Breeding long-haired rabbits. *Crossing Chickens With Success*. But Mina enjoyed describing the process, and Mother considered that to be part of the lesson.

You may be imagining that Mother was older than Mina, but this was not the case. Mina was a widower whose husband had drowned when his fishing boat capsized on the river. His buddy, Chuck, had also drowned, fishing and drinking being complements only until swimming is required. Mina's husband had made her life so miserable that after he was buried, she reverted to her maiden name and title as if to erase her blighted conjugal past. She was nearly fifty when she took over the bookmobile. This was during Mother's history-of-medicine phase, and it was six months before Mina realized that Mother was not the first female doctor she'd ever met. "No, dear Miss Mina," Mother had laughed, "I am not a physician. Just interested in infections and why anyone ever imagined that leeches were a solution. Of course in time our children's children will probably scoff at talk therapy and shudder at our use of antibiotics."

As the freezing rain picked up, Mina became visibly anxious, and Mother cut short her browsing.

"I'm sure these will keep me occupied till next time. I hate to keep you here in this weather."

"You're too kind, Ms. Washington. But I promised to hold

a book for Mrs. Kilpatrick, so I can't leave before she arrives."

"Oh, dear, Miss Mina, there's no way you could have heard. The Kilpatricks lost their daughter two weeks ago. Ms. Alanis took it very hard, understandably, and has gone to Woodhaven for help."

"So sad. So terribly sad. Why do such things happen?"

"That's been a common question around here for the past month, Miss Mina. The only answer, unsatisfying as it may be, is 'No reason—they just do.' And we endure."

I blushed, as did Miss Wilhelmina, but for different reasons. I have always been proud of Mother, but her philosophizing embarrassed me to the same degree that it flummoxed our neighbors. Miss Mina flipped awkwardly through Alanis Kilpatrick's book.

"Is that Jane Austen?" Mother asked. She reached over the counter and took the book from Miss Mina. "*Emma.* Probably better for mind and soul than anything at Woodhaven, no offense to her therapists. I know it's un-orthodox, Miss Mina, but let me deliver this to her. Even if she can't read it now, it's a letter from the world outside her sorrow. That can't hurt."

If Miss Mina was troubled by this rule-bending—the book could not be officially checked out without Alanis' card—the rattle of sleet on the metal roof of the bookmobile signaled a worsening storm and a greater source of worry than backlash from the circulation librarian. She thanked Mother, who also took out *The Poetry of Rumi* for Alanis, and the bookmobile waddled cautiously onto the road as Mother and I scraped the windshield of the station wagon and prepared to leave.

"Miss Wilhelmina Greene is a good egg," Mother declared. "And Austen is the perfect author to help Alanis escape her troubles. Smart escapism, mind you. So brilliant. Have you read Austen, Sol? And don't you say Austen is for girls because that's ignorant. Is Melville only for boys? And James Baldwin...only if you're black and gay?"

I had not read Austen, but neither had I heard she was only for girls. People said that of Alcott, but Mother read me *Eight Cousins* and *Little Women* when I was in elementary school so that I would love Jo before it became queer. Mother's efforts to forestall the narrow-mindedness prized as truth by our community were the hallmark of her parenting. She was strategic, perspicacious, and sometimes original. She never did anything so trite as give me a doll. Rather she taught me, at six, to change my sister Joan's diaper. On July 4th we did not grill hamburgers and hotdogs. Mother made tamales or curry and recited Emma Lazarus. Although she had been a member of Shelburne Baptist her whole life and we attended faithfully every Sunday, on Wednesday evenings we drove into Lewisburg for the Unitarians' spiritual study group. As the first born, I predictably complied with Mother's efforts and was the strangest kid in my class. But I was always accepted as such. Only new kids snickered at my name, Solomon Descartes Washington, or looked askance at my lunches of granola or tapioca. By my teen years, I had learned when to hold my strangeness in reserve and when to deploy it to my advantage. After all, one is only odd or common in context. Mother's gift to us was that she set us on a path elsewhere while equipping us to be tolerant and exceptional here.

Mother's willfulness, however, could be blinding. Her devotion to a cause could turn into much of a muchness that swept everyone up and hurled us onward whether we liked it or not. With sleet pelting down and rain crystallizing on barbed wire fences along the road, Mother decided to drive to Woodhaven to deliver the books to Alanis Kilpatrick. In balance with Alanis' needs, the weather was a minor inconvenience to her. Mother had been driving for twenty years without incident. Why worry today when a few extra minutes would put the book in Alanis' hands? If the temperature dropped, conditions would be worse tomorrow, and then what would we do? No doubt become inert, hesitate again, and in a week's time, those books would still be on our kitchen table, inducing guilt, multiplied daily by our failed good intentions. "It's how we come to resent doing favors," Mother explained as we fishtailed up a hill. "Procrastination becomes guilt, guilt becomes resentment, and soon we have blamed someone for being in need even though she never asked for our help."

"But won't the same thing happen if we slide off into the ditch?"

"No, because we are above that, Sol. And because we won't slide into a ditch."

The road to Woodhaven is a favorite Sunday drive. A renovated Georgian mansion, built in 1840, serves as the institution's main building, and the five-mile approach was once a carriageway carefully landscaped to afford favorable views. The modern road followed the carriageway through a canopy of Dutch elms before the beetle wiped them out, and it still winds along a creek and a fence of stacked stone. Even in the ice storm, and despite my anxiety, I succumbed momentarily to the lovely image of black angus cows huddled close under a towering red oak, its leaves glazed and limbs refusing to sag. Mother brought me back to reality. She could not drive this road without explaining that we weren't looking at nature but at "Nature." She would then implore me to remember that enslaved black people cleared the timber for these pastures, shoveled the fill dirt to make the road bank along the creek bed, and hauled each and every stone of the fence that now shimmered in our head-lights. "If you can't hear them suffering when your heart is stirred by this or that prospect, you need to listen harder," she would say.

The last argument that I recall her having with my father was on this topic. He loved autumn, and during his final months with cancer, Mother indulged him in a drive through the elms. There was a breeze, the trees showered gold all over the car and across the road. My father sighed. Mother couldn't stop herself. She had the grace to murmur, but not enough to remain silent or be so quiet as to go unheard. "It was always about gold," she said. My father, who was wrapped in a blanket and wore a knit cap despite the Indian summer heat, lurched forward. He wheezed, his chest rattled, and he began to cough that profound, rib-shattering cough of lungs enflamed and desperate for oxygen. Mother pulled over and ran around to the passenger door. She opened it just as my father vomited. He grabbed at Mother to steady himself, and she rubbed his back as he coughed and vomited again into the ditch. The leaves swirled around them and the coughing went on and on. I recall that too vividly, how you would think the end was in sight, there would be a lull, then again would come the rattle that presaged a renewed fit. By the time this ended, and you could hear the creek babbling and a red-winged blackbird declaring its territory, Mother was in tears and whispering over and over, "I'm sorry, Frank. I'm so, so sorry." It's the only argument she had ever lost to him, in the only way that she could lose.

Delivering the books to Woodhaven ended up being anti-climactic. Mother was right that Alanis would be pleased to receive the books. We were allowed to speak to her briefly, and Mother later explained that it was probably the valium that made her so placid. Mother was also right that the car would not slide off the road. The trouble came as it always does, ingloriously and unpredictably, even though it makes sense in our family's narrative. This, too, I learned from Mother. Stories are retrospective and sensible. Life is present and unaccountable.

Mother had let Joan stay home from Nora Hopkins' funeral. Joan was 14, didn't know Nora very well, and ever since our father's death had been disturbed to sleeplessness by open caskets. She teared up when she asked Mother to excuse her, and while tears were never enough to convince Mother, her recent history with Joan led her to predict a battle if she refused. In the balance, it really didn't matter if Joan missed the funeral. Mother made her promise to stay indoors and prep the dinner vegetables.

Joan never fit well between Mother and me. She was the piece that came with the puzzle but had to be trimmed to make it stay in place. Our father's death sharpened her oblique angles. I was not close to him. I loved and grieved for him, but not in the way Joan did. Although our father never demonstrated a preference for either of us, she had made him her parent, since it was clear that Mother and I were a pair. When he died, the sorrow welled up in her as if from some dark lake deep inside. She wept daily for so long that her sixth grade teacher suggested a psychiatric evaluation—a suggestion that Mother responded to by moving Joan to another class. Then, abruptly, the crying gave way to the vacant expression of one who knows that she is forever outnumbered and misapprehended. Joan withdrew, became quiet and docile, until adolescence, when evidence of her difference began to reemerge, mostly in the form of challenges to Mother's values. She quit dance, concert band, and Latin, all under duress. She argued her way out of confirmation class on the reasonable grounds that Mother was a skeptic, had taught her to be skeptical, and could not expect her to learn anything new from Pastor John, a Biblical literalist. A prolonged engagement over the question of piercings—Mother forbid more than one in each lobe—deteriorated into a week of sullen silence, followed by Joan's return from a sleepover with a stud in her right nostril, left eyebrow, and belly button. These were do-it-yourself jobs with straight pins and shots of peach Schnapps. Joan was grounded for a month but did not otherwise suffer ill

144

effects from drunkenness or infections from her friend's unsterile needlework.

Détente was an overused noun in the news during that period, but it aptly described the state that Mother and daughter entered when the grounding was lifted. Joan rejoined band, maintained her grades, and engaged in civil if innocuous conversation at supper. It could hardly be doubted that she secretly carried on activities that Mother would disapprove of. But Mother, for her part, did not probe. I imagine that she had resolved to respond only to overt defiance or careless disclosure of wrongdoing. When Joan asked to stay home from Nora's funeral, Mother had no grounds for suspicion and good reason to accede to her daughter's request.

The power was out when we finally turned onto our street after the Woodhaven trip. What little light there had been from the late afternoon was now snuffed by the storm and nightfall. Mother hadn't worried about Joan before now even though reason might have had her worrying an hour earlier, rather than as we approached the house. But in the blackout, with the downpour of sleet and rain, it was impossible to be philosophical. When she turned off the headlights, we might have been suspended in a cavern, the brown noise that filled our ears being the flapping of bats' wings. Mother had decided to park at the foot of our long, steep driveway for fear of getting the car stuck in the middle. To me, getting stuck was a risk preferable to being soaked in cold rain before entering a house without heat. I said as much to Mother. It was too dark to see her expression, but I felt it. Her response was, "You lead the way. Your eyes are younger than mine, and you're sure-footed."

Mother had had the driveway paved over the summer. Climbing it in dress shoes, with Mother clinging to my shoulder, was skating uphill, a slow doddery affair with frequent unintended tangents and spins. Without the downpour, and perhaps with a functioning floodlight from our house, this might have been funny, at least in hindsight. Instead it was ominous. There is a dream that I have every time I am sick. I'm running a race, and with maximum effort I only manage to inch along. I realize that I'm on my hands and knees, then pulling myself along on my belly. Runners dash by obliviously, and I shudder that all my training has come to this, but it's all I can do to drag my body toward an invisible finish line. Pulling Mother along in the dark was like being inside that dream.

"Joan, dear?" Mother called when we finally reached the porch and opened the door. The house was hollow and voiceless, the loss of electricity having squelched the lowgrade hums and buzzes we associate with silence. No candles had been lit, so I took a flashlight from the front hall closet. From the entrance of our small house, every room was visible: living room, kitchen, three bedrooms and a bathroom. The light scanned them as Mother continued to call and get no answer. By the stove, there was a mound of chopped carrots and celery. At least Joan had fulfilled that promise before leaving.

"I'll phone Lydia's. She probably got scared and walked over there." When Mother suppressed her worry, her voice took on a jovial exasperation. The only quality more out of character would have been blind fury, which I doubt she ever experienced. She laughed and sighed when she picked up the phone. It gave me goosebumps.

Lydia was my father's only living sibling. She adored Joan and me, she abhorred Mother. "She complicates simple things," Aunt Lydia would say. She had been a teenager when my father was born, so she was much older than Mother, whom she considered to be arrested in youthful impracticality and self-absorption. I could see why she thought that, but it wasn't fair. What Aunt Lydia lacked in intellectual curiosity she made up for in homespun wisdom of the kind that Mother did not respect. Aunt Lydia said things like, "Cross that bridge when you get to it," and "A wise man don't bite the hand that feeds him," and "The Lord works in mysterious ways." She cross-stitched samplers with such aphorisms and hung them throughout the house. She was Mother's opposite in almost every way. She was a huge woman who baked cakes from boxes. She voted for Reagan and gave money to Christian radio. She agreed with Mother's objections to Joan's rebelliousness and piercings, but she blamed Mother's overbearing ways for both.

Having raised my father, Aunt Lydia considered herself more advanced than Mother in rearing our family's children even though she had none of her own. "I never had kids but I raised your father and know that boys will be boys," she would declare. "Because I raised your father, who was sometimes a handful, I know that children must experiment." "In my experience rearing your father, it never paid to punish too harshly. The punishment must fit the crime." That was Aunt Lydia's unsolicited response when Mother grounded Joan, as if she wouldn't have done more had my father gone the way of the hippies.

Unsurprisingly the phone lines had snapped under the weight of the ice, so we slid back down the driveway, intending to drive to Aunt Lydia's. But when we reached the car, her four-wheel drive pickup rumbled up behind us. The heat of the exhaust quickly formed a cloud around the idling truck. When Aunt Lydia stepped out, we could see Joan hunched up in the passenger's seat.

"Why, Lydia, we were just about to drive over. I am so relieved Joan had you to turn to. She must have been worried." Mother was sincere, even if graciousness dictated such a greeting.

Aunt Lydia looked like the Gorton's fisherman in her vast trench coat and sou'wester. She had taken to walking with a cane, and leaned on it now. "It's hard to believe we had crocuses peeking out just last week. Pneumonia weather," she declared, as if small talk were in order despite the freezing drizzle.

"So they say. I parked the car down here for fear of getting it stuck on the driveway. You'd not be worried about that in your truck, of course. I'll move my car and you can pull on up and come in. We'll build a fire."

Aunt Lydia's face was invisible under the brim of her hat, but I know that her eyes narrowed and her lips pursed. That was always the expression she assumed before coming to the point. "We won't be staying, Muriel. We've come for a few of Joan's things. Clothes and such. Sometimes a niece just needs her auntie, and I've welcomed her to stay with me as long as she needs to."

Mother's voice again assumed that unnatural joviality. "Let's just all head inside, get warmed up, and chat. I recommend you drive up. I worry about your slipping on the ice."

Lydia was firm. "Muriel, there's a season for all things. Joanie needs her auntie. We'll talk when she's ready."

"Lydia, I know that you love my children and mean

well. But I really must insist that we talk this over now, in a rational way, inside, when we are warm and dry."

"Muriel, my gear has me plenty dry, and the cab of my truck is toasty. Joanie is fine there while I get her things. Only reason she came along at all was she wanted to stick close to her auntie."

Mother and Aunt Lydia stared at each other. Neither would be the first to flinch. In elementary school, we played a game with the black rubber combs we carried in our hip pockets. Your opponent made a fist, and bending your comb back as far as it would go without breaking, you snapped him across the knuckles. If your aim was true, the teeth gouged little bloody trenches. The trick was that you and your opponent stared at each other through the whole proceedings. Your opponent could pull away, but he couldn't blink. That was flinching. Mother and Aunt Lydia would have emerged wide-eyed and fingerless from such a contest.

The only mercy in those few moments was that the ice stopped falling. We were left with the raw wetness, there in the scarlet glow of Aunt Lydia's taillights and the thickening putrescence of diesel exhaust. I caught Joan's eyes. They were swollen from her crying. The stud in her eyebrow looked cankerous. She was swallowed up in Aunt Lydia's blanket, a fleece decorated with Disney characters. At the time I had no inkling of what could have upset her so.

Certainly not having been alone in the storm. And yet even a stranger could have seen that she just wanted to disappear. I started up the driveway.

"Sol, where are you going?" Mother asked.

I didn't pause. "You and Aunt Lydia stay put. I'll toss a few clothes into Joan's duffel bag and be back in a minute." Mother objected, but I ignored her. I slipped and stumbled back to the house. When Mother tells this story, she makes Joan into a prodigal daughter and me into the favored elder son, but one who was disobedient rather than envious. If I had been true to the archetype, I would have hovered quietly in the red cloud until Mother successfully stared Aunt Lydia into submission. My aberrant move so flummoxed Mother that she lost the upper hand. During my absence, she actually wept. Lydia's triumph was assured, and I was to blame.

Entering my sister's room with a flashlight was like spelunking. Joan collected mobiles. Biplanes, skiers, exotic shells, and safari animals dangled from the ceiling. None of Joan's clothes were in drawers. There were colorful piles mixing the recently washed and thoroughly soiled, with no distinction between outer and under wear. Her walls were better organized. Each was a separate shrine to Joey Ramone, Morrisey, Blondie, and the X-Men. My flashlight glinted on Deborah Harry's striped jumper. "When I met you in the restaurant, you could tell I was no debutante." The gold shag rug was filthy with crumbs. Mother left it to us to clean our rooms, and it had been part of Joan's deviance to ignore chores. Her bed was piled with school books, photo albums, and magazines, and in the middle, her pink phone was off the hook.

The phone had been a surprising concession to Joan's adolescent wishes. It required a separate line and a financial outlay that Mother would normally dismiss as a bourgeois American extravagance. But turning the gift into an opportunity to teach Joan fiscal responsibility, Mother garnished Joan's babysitting earnings to offset the line charges. Right now the phone was dead because the lines were down, but just as I reached to replace the handset, the lights flickered and the house began to whir and mutter with electricity. Joan's answering machine, a bulky cassette deck on her nightstand, rewound and began to play. I recognized the voice of her friend, Anita.

"Joan, with the ice and all, Darlene says she can't take you for the thing today. So sorry. Try not to worry! Can you get free tomorrow?"

There was a pause, a beep, then another message. The voice this time was male. I didn't recognize it.

"Joan? It's me. Pick up. Is it done? Don't be mysterious. Pick up."

Another pause, another beep, and Anita again.

"Joan. Darlene says erase that. She means my message. She's being paranoid. This one too, she says. God, Darlene, shut up! Anyway, you probably should erase it. I'm so sorry, Joan. Tomorrow. Darlene says it's quick. God, Darlene, shut up already. Did Darrell call? Tell him fuck off if he does because he tried here, that loser. Okay, so erase this so Darlene will…"

The last one was the boy again. Darrell.

"Joan. I know Darlene's a skank, but you have to go with her. Pick up. Don't be mysterious. Call me."

I was 19 that winter, taking a year off to work so I could pay tuition. I wasn't very experienced in love, but I had friends and an imagination. Even still, I would not have pieced together my sister's story from these fragments had it not been for the photo album next to the phone. It was not one of Joan's private compendiums of roller rink snapshots and movie tickets. It was a family album opened to a page of Polaroids of Mother when she was pregnant with Joan.

In the South, snow and ice do not linger. By the end of the week, temperatures reached 70, and sun lit the labor of everyone who had chain saws and pick-up trucks. There was so much to clean up that nobody warned of pneumonia weather. Mother and I made our weekly sojourn to the graveyard to freshen my father's flowers. Miss Wilhelmina

Green was there. Even her ne'er-do-well late husband deserved a tidy plot, as all the dead do.

"Ms. Washington, I see you survived the ice storm. I was worried sick after you left the bookmobile. Conditions were dreadful! I said a little prayer."

"Miss Mina, I have no doubt that your prayer helped. In fact, it got us all the way to Woodhaven and back with barely a slip."

"Oh my goodness gracious! You did not deliver that book in the ice? You are intrepid!"

Mother smiled.

"Is your little Joan well? I haven't seen her with you lately."

Mother had prepared responses to this question to suit a range of interrogators. To Miss Mina, she replied, "She's enjoying her aunt's company for a few days while the schools are still closed."

"Oh how nice! Sometimes a girl just needs her auntie."

Mother nodded and began to address my father's grave. The storm had littered the plot with twigs, and the pot of mums had scattered. We gathered all this and carried it to a compost heap in the edge of the woods. Then Mother brought a fresh basket of purple mums from the car. She also brought a hammer and three tomato stakes. She drove a stake through the plastic base of each basket and up to the hilt in the potting soil, anchoring all of them to the grave. She said nothing through all of this. She was completely focused. I just watched her.

Later we would go to Aunt Lydia's, and Mother would again fail to persuade Joan to return home. Adding insult to injury, she would learn that Aunt Lydia had convinced Joan to keep the baby. "There is no reason nowadays to continue an unwanted pregnancy," she would declare as Lydia showed us the door. "The real tragedy is the ruining of a young girl's future."

But for now we marveled at the sturdiness of Mother's mums even as the wind picked up. No change in the weather, however dramatic, would tip over the flowers on my father's grave. And on the drive to Aunt Lydia's, I read aloud from *Pride and Prejudice*, the scene where Elizabeth refuses Darcy. That changes him. You could also say that it's the beginning of her change, too.

Mind of Winter Revisited

(for SRF)

A cube, suspended, each side peeling away slowly, creating thin squares, whose souls, themselves squares of all sizes, dislodge and drift, leaving frames that now in the slight breeze off the cold river begin to spiral, whirling like skaters along the ice, and the squares, their souls, are multi-colored apparitions that shadow them, undulating along the lines inscribed by the gay helixes, cast in the clear light of winter periodically fractured by sheets of blackbirds but never fully obscured, for a single bird will peel off, dark star, unruly and exuberant, opening the way for an arc of light such that the ice, now scarified and dusted with minute crystalline shavings, exhales foggy rainbows whose shape, shifting, the snow-feathered boy sets out to imagine.

AM Radio

Losing the signal.

Sibilants and plosives hiss and pop excessively.

A low susurrant continuo,
the ground,
swells,
a rising wind across sand dunes,
an unending exhalation,

an open ellipsis,
its promise, that great gettin' up mornin',
or perhaps the space within the ellipsis,
unarticulated and understood,
where now does not involve next.

Whether to turn the knob

.

Slow Leaves

Llega el invierno. Espléndido dictado
me dan las lentas hojas
vestidas de silencio y amarillo.
--Pablo Neruda, "El jardin invierno"

Clothed in silence, my grandmother has wandered into a dark forest from which there is no return. Whether she knows where she is or what she is doing there—whether she is doing or knowing anything at all—we can't say. On rare occasions, under the unnaturally clear light of a hospital room, her eyes open slightly, but without the wonder or bewilderment of an infant's sporadic wakefulness. My mother, who retired after thirty years as an elementary school teacher's aide, spends most days and many nights by her mother's bedside. When prompted to drink—the prompt consists of a verbal command and a cup to her lips—Grandma will drink a honeyed, protein-and-lipid-infused beverage called Glucerna. To consume a few ounces can take her more than an hour. I've watched my mother hold the cup to her mother's lips, coax and praise her, and tell her the latest family news. My mother's voice is bright. Her arm never quivers.

To pass the time, my mother sings, much as she sang to my brother and me when we were sick. She sings hymns, full of blood and grace, hymns incised so deeply in the heart of a Baptist as to rival the autonomic script for breathing. The woods are too dark for Grandma to see her way clear, but maybe she hears "Softly and Tenderly" and "I'll Fly Away" in a familiar voice.

Staying under such circumstances requires a degree of generosity that I could not fathom before I became a parent. Even now, I must confess that I glance anxiously at my watch while keeping vigil by the sick. True generosity knows no regret. The clock winds down unnoticed.

Whose voice was that? I am in a parlor, dimly lit. It smells of hickory and rosewater. My great grandmother, Pantha James, is dressed for company—not my company, but that of dead ancestors and friends. She has pulled her silver hair back in elaborate twists, rouged and powdered her aging cheeks to disguise the webs of capillaries. She is a poor farmer's wife but once reminded my mother, "We are ladies," as they painted the nails on their callused hands.

Wet from the rain in my walk from the school bus, I clutch my book satchel and hover quietly in the shadows by the front door. I'm afraid of interrupting. She is talking to Reuben, a favorite uncle, who fought in the Civil War and returned to start the local Baptist church. She speaks the language of the dead, which is like the language of sleepwalkers, inflected and energetic. The phrases sound familiar but prove unintelligible in the waking world. She pauses when he responds, mutters approval or disapproval and, very often, laughs aloud, for he is a man with a wicked sense of humor. Farmer preachers often are, and having been baptized in the blood of neighbors at the Battle of the Wilderness, Reuben came to appreciate the salvific effect of levity. I of course cannot hear his jokes. The punch lines are delivered below the threshold of hearing.

Espléndido dictado, firelight on the wet window panes, a dance of little demons, erratic, unpredictable. An aged mind with its unnameable affliction gathers the dead into the world of the living. "Don't laugh at me," she scolds, her gaze suddenly luminous and bearing down on me. I haven't laughed, and I say so, mortified. But her eyes have dimmed already. She returns to her twilight conversation.

Winter arrives. Bitten by the wind, the body won't be ignored. Coat, hat, gloves, and a brisk pace: protection, concentration, motion, nothing is enough. Your thoughts grow cold. And then there interposes a sound, "Some glad morning when this life is o'er," grainy and distant, growing loud as a laugh or Dickinson's bluebottle in the death chamber, "with Blue—uncertain stumbling Buzz." From the splendid dictation of a fulfilled life, something not quite forgotten, the rustle of automatic writing, slow leaves across the mind of the dying.

Hockey Puck

So little friction.

Like the soul (which only knows itself because the body
slips into the cold air and strikes the surface,)
it aspires to the condition of light:

                              it would not be outpaced,

                              it would bank around and move

beyond

                              unslowed.

But in this world bodies stop

                    "The car began to glide into the path of a UPS

truck and all I

                    could think was 'I'll never see Jon and Delia

again.'"

short of the edge the soul seeks.

Portrait of Betsy

Like a postcard

It was, in fact, a cottage nestled in a bower of lilac and elms. Had it been an imitation only, the actualization of an ideal that she assembled from her collection of Book-of-the-Month club historical romances, those refinished English landscapes, Wessex Americanized with more optimism and light, might its effect have been different, shallower, as when you know that the fog-shrouded Icelandic fishing village in the feature film was staged in Maine? Only if she had not lived there and in May trained the yellow antique roses up the trellis over her walkway to the door, which was nothing fancy, screen and painted pine milled at the river. Free of poor farmstead rubbish, unapologetically manicured, her house stood out among the homes in our village, a postcard among Depression-era photos, lavender and carnation against a background of browns, grease and manure. It seemed elsewhere but was not. She lived there, at the end of a gravel road, or more accurately, a lane. You could see her through the rippled glass of the picture window. In the front room, off the parlor, she made dolls.

Were You There?

"Sometimes it causes me to tremble," she sang, and the lyric seemed to come from inside not just her but us, the tremble was not mere vibrato, but an effect of the lyric's tones, an unanticipated dip in the body's core temperature, welling up from the organs and spreading along the skin like breath on a cold windshield, the way one's suffering becomes another's. As when her husband, a quiet man, was killed in a car on a winter evening, and we stood in her dark parlor with the grandchildren, we were small, there were Barbies to play with, you could hear the wind and someone whispered, "She's talking out of her mind so they've given her pills." Sometimes it causes me to tremble. Imagine thorns, the preacher would say, like those as big as a child's thumb that thicken in double, triple helixes among the pines near the river, shoved into the flesh of your forehead, like the bursting glass that rendered her beloved unrecognizable so they kept the coffin closed. Sometimes it should cause me to tremble, she sang, but I cannot. I have borne enough, my stillness is absolute, I'm not sure my heart beats, there's no ringing in my ears.

Graveyard Encounter

Back from the river, past the fox tracks and the bone shards of a gosling that didn't make it to the water on time, under the vinca, thick, tangled, and unkempt, there are gravestones. Names and dates eroded away long ago, years after someone leaned here on a shovel, the sun dripping on the water like the autumn trees around him, the minutes gathering towards his own descent.

I went in search of the gravestones and found them attended by the ghost of a boy. I knew him to be a ghost because of the way he carried himself—with the light but dignified air of one who has crossed over—and because on the surface of his eyes, scenes from local history were continuously playing. He was thin and dark and completely at ease with my interrogations. It was near dusk after a rain on a sweltering midsummer day. The ebbing light was trapped in streaks of steam. The ghost caught at these and wound them around his hand and elbow like rope.

I apologized for interrupting his work and asked if he knew the names of the people in the graves. He smiled sympathetically and a series of faces passed across the surface of his eyes. Among them was a toddler with a tiny, pursed mouth, and a man over whose left eye there was a heavy scar that made him appear to squint. I knew them both. But I asked their names, hoping to press the ghost into speech. He blinked, and in his left eye I watched the toddler's body convulsing, and in his right the man's body being pulled from the water.

"Why show me how they ended?" I asked, for I had always objected to identifying my people with when and how they died. His response was to hand me the end of his sun rope and motion me towards the river. The rope was warm and heavy, and he fed me lengths of it while I held it like a tether and descended to the bank. On the river's surface were reflected imposing violet cloud formations left over from the rainstorm, flecked with the scarlet of the lowering sun. As I watched, these formations became the walls of the celestial city, and I walked out into the water and stood at the foot of a great stairway. The rope grew taut, I couldn't let go, and against my will I was pulled back to the bank and up the hill. My ankles caught and tangled in the vinca, I fell roughly against the blunted edge of the buried stones. Angry, I called for the ghost boy, but he had gone. The rope dissipated into the cooling air.

For the day was now departing. Crouching, the sun hissed and an alarm went up from the whippoorwills, they who at every departure forecast doom even as they delight in their feast of mosquitoes. I looked back and there were few traces of my having passed this way, though the path was strewn with the lumber of so many travelers that in truth I couldn't distinguish what was mine from yours or theirs. "Best not mess around in all that," Father once said, "else you'll get onto a snake."

The hiss became a sigh. The whippoorwills swooped and ate in silence. Dusk is a peacemaker but not one to linger. The light went out. I wasn't sure of my next step.

Owls

I. Before daybreak, a great horned owl speaks

He did not equivocate.

What he knew could not be gainsaid, and what he said—

Singular, from the base of his barrel chest—

Rang with a buoy's prophetic conviction

When I, running in the dark, caught sight of a skunk

Who crossed ahead, elegant ambler, too sure of his defenses.

Surveying the scatter of inhabited worlds,

The lord arranges a path to his desire.

He will arrive when he pleases, and the wind,

Proverbially, will be at his back, his wings

silent as their shadows.

What age, unwitting, under what dawn,

Receives him, his talons a sudden directive,

His yellow eye a concentration of no one's hope?

So this becomes a poem about empires, or gods, or death,

Loses sight of the owl, hidden and watchful, the arc

Of his understanding, his earless tufts, his hunger,

And the skunk, who may or may not have felt

That bass note or his spine snap

Beneath the parallel, perfect white stripes.

II. Dream (After Goya's *El sueño de la razón produce monstruos*)

The owls surrounded me while my reason slept: the chief translator, with his indignant glare; the sympathetic one, his wings outspread; and the prophet, hunched in terror. A giant, his face too deep in the night sky to be detected, could not sweep them away, despite his hand, the breadth of a mainsail. The owls were agile, and even the calluses of a giant's fingers could not withstand their talons.

"Much of what I say," screeched the translator upon returning, "you will ignore even if you understand it."

"Everyone does," said the sympathetic one. "Ask the prophet."

The moon struggled and failed, so except for the lantern that dangled from the giant's distant earlobe, there was no light. Dimness sharpens concentration, as the cat that lay behind me knew best of all. Equally agile in dark and light, mystery to everything but herself, in silence she watched and listened.

"That one," the prophet rumbled, "devours the meek and catches the wise one off-guard. In the play of her tail, mark the shifting balance."

"Who can keep his eye trained on that tail and not be mesmerized?" the second owl protested. "Best to look beyond her while maintaining the strength to respond."

"Hear the words of the giant," screeched the translator. " 'My appetite will not go unsatisfied.'"

The cat's tail was a slow serpent of smoke. It was a drifting river under dark branches from which depend spectral fingers of moss, helix on helix in the night breeze, the giant's breath that levitated the owls.

"Keep your eyes shut," whispered the sympathetic one close by my ear.

The Marsh

("Ecstasy," Sacred Harp 106)

Oh, when shall I see Jesus,
And reign with Him above?
And from the flowing fountain
Drink everlasting love?

Charon shoves off, the duckweed and lilies gripping the sides of our bark as if to hold it to the shore. He digs deep with his pole, and we have soon drifted to the center of the marsh, where decaying trees thrive, swathed in hungry moss and millipedes. Yellow warblers kindle the mist. This is not a space of dead souls even if it is strewn with carcasses, sloughed off cicada exoskeletons, the wreckage of seasons and last days.

On the bank behind us is a man in khaki with a camera and an enormous telephoto lens. He ignores us, because the slosh of the bow has driven the startled warblers closer to him. Besides, he's already taken the requisite photo of us. The birds have filled a honeysuckle vine, and he shoots repeatedly. The shutter's sound reminds us of the sand blocks you play in Kindergarten orchestras. As we cross over, it fades into the percussion symphony of the marsh, led by the cicadas.

Their noise, a vigorous rattling, speeds into an electronic quaver then shatters into rings and small bells. Persistent as tinnitus, it won't resolve into a single key, the bright accessible C or even the more demanding C#. I called it "noise," but when you tap your foot regularly to keep from being frightened—we are crossing over, after all—doesn't it become music? Maybe this is the music of eternity. One note, crescendo, decrescendo, repeat. If the dead, cabined and buried, could detect the thump on the ear drum and rattling of the ossicular chain, something like this would be what they hear underground. The sound of the earth spinning.

And yet maybe I have it all wrong. The rattle and quaver are rhythm for a jubilee of piping, croaking, and cawing. Think New Orleans street funerals, every alley full of vibrato and ecstasy, music bridging the otherwise silent plain between this world and the next. Standing in the bow, listening to the jubilee, watching the cameraman dissolve in the mists, it is not impossible to feel transported.

Or to be overwhelmed, you point out. All that sound

bears down on us just as the earth will when we reach the other side. The passage between ecstasy and dread is short, a semitone away. It's harder to rise back up. "An horrible drede hath overwhelmed me," sang the Psalmist, "Oh that I had wynges like a dove, that I might fle somewhere and be at rest."

We are not doves, nor are we borne on a dove's wings. To be overwhelmed is to have no real hope of flight. Consider the word and our little boat. Inside "overwhelm," deep inside it, is "whelve," to cover over or turn upside down. Deeper still is "hwealf." That is an arch or vault—the sky above us—and also the V-shape of our bark from gunwales to centerline. The very shape of our boat is synonymous with its capsizing. We are whelved as we flee somewhere to be at rest, and we are whelved if we stand in the bow beneath the sky filled with this unending death rattle. And one other etymological curiosity: hwealf is kin to the Gothic hwilfri, a coffin, our final vessel, lowered in a vault and whelved in earth.

If I'm not mistaken, our boatman just nodded.

Oh had I wings, I would
Fly away and be at rest,
And praise God in his bright abode.

When a dove flees a barrage of pellets fired off by autumn's eager hunters, his wings whistle an alarm. A flock of doves taking flight from a mown field is a frantic chorus of staccato whistles, air raid, air raid, flee for cover from the brawny white man, orange-capped, vested in camouflage, and strapped together with belts of red and green cartridges.

He shoots repeatedly.

Some fall into the marsh and sink, breasts heavy with lead. It's as if we're being shelled by manna as we cross over. Remember what the preacher said: God is so generous that those doves for the Israelites in the wilderness probably came with hushpuppies under one wing and tartar sauce under the other.

Fly away and be at rest.

Always in a minor key, the dove's call consists of five notes. The first swoops up six steps to a grace note and lands on a perfect fifth. Then follow three slow, repeated statements, one whole step above the tonic: imagine A to an appoggiatura F onto E, then B, B, B. Breathy, distant, and unresolved, it is the archetypal sound of loneliness.

Between each call is a whole rest, sometimes with fermata. The mourning dove has mastered the use of silence. "That I might fle somewhere and be at rest": for example inside the dove's call, between the measures. The little black rectangle in the middle of the staff, that is your makeshift pillow, under the watchful eye of the fermata. You will be like Jacob in flight, resting his head on a stone, under the gaze of Yahweh.

Gird on the gospel armor
Of faith and hope and love,
And when the combat's ended,
He'll carry you above.

Lethargic, Charon lets the boat drift. Night threatens. The photographer has vanished. The guns have stopped. A fog rolls in, viscous and opaque.

"Light a candle," our boatman sighs.

The darkness splinters and reassembles around a feeble halo. Dust motes flutter through like cherubim, sickly, disoriented. You reach for one but he disappears into the mist.

The other shore—who can see it? We will run aground in time.

You laugh. We are not "in time" any longer, you say.

But what of the impending nightfall, and the fact that we move forward, if at a snail's pace? No, we are not yet out of time, either. The clock still applies. We will stay under its rule until the shore, beyond which there is no time. When we disembark, a guide will meet us. He holds a lantern and will lead us to our end.

How do I know these things, you ask? Have you considered the alternative? We are met only by darkness. No guide, no light. Our footing unsure, the muddy shore slipping away beneath us, we stumble forward until we strike stones or dry land. The wind that now blows the fog in, it will only worsen, grow louder than the cicadas whose music we'll wish we could hear. Overwhelmed, how could we possibly move without a guide?

We must gird our loins. Faith, hope, and love…we had these always, we have them still. If we are put on shore together, we will surely find our way. If not we will hold each other.

In the distance, a faint green lantern flickers. Will o the wisp with the wings of a dove.

Oh had I wings, I would
Fly away and be at rest,
And praise God in his bright abode.

Artist's Statement

When faced with the task of illustrating Derek's Semitones, I couldn't help but to think how my illustrations would be able to convey the almost infinite, fleeting images that Derek's words evoked in my mind.

The answer seemed to be that each medium has its own abilities, strengths and weaknesses, just like the rest of us.

But another consideration came to the surface as well. "Are images and language the only ways of communicating on paper? Could there be other unexplored ones?"

And perhaps because I couldn't come up with a new way all on my own, I decided to experiment with mixing both. Or perhaps I might come up with a completely original means of creating: the image-word.

Is it possible to write and draw at the same time?

I tried. I took Derek's stories and drew with them. What appeared on the page is neither the original writing nor a typical image, but something with that fleeting quality evoked by the reading.

It is rather the norm today to mix mediums in art. The

results are often uncomfortable but hopefully help us grow.

And though my experiment proved rather difficult, with some effort and a bunch of "it's a process" reminders, I came up with these illustrations.

Andrés San Millán

Andrés and his wife Marguerite are the founders and artistic directors of Cocoon Theatre in Poughkeepsie, NY.

Fomite

A fomite is a medium capable of transmitting infectious organisms from one individual to another.

"The activity of art is based on the capacity of people to be infected by the feelings of others." Tolstoy, *What Is Art?*

Writing a review on Amazon, Good Reads, Shelfari, Library Thing or other social media sites for readers will help the progress of independent publishing. To submit a review, go to the book page on any of the sites and follow the links for reviews. Books from independent presses rely on reader to reader communications.

For more information or to order any of our books, visit http://www.fomitepress.com/FOMITE/Our_Books.html

*The Moment
Before an Injury*
Joshua Amses

*Nothing Beside
Remains*
Jaysinh Birjépatil

*The Way None
of This Happened*
Mike Breiner

Victor Rand
David Brizer

*Summer on the
Cold War Planet*
Paula Closson Buck

*Cycling in Plato's
Cave*
David Cavanagh

Fomite

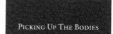

Picking Up the Bodies
James F. Connolly

Unfinished Stories of Girls
Catherine Zobal Dent

Drawing on Life
Mason Drukman

Free Fall/Caída libre
Tina Escaja

Foreign Tales of Exemplum and Woe
J. C. Ellefson

Sinfonia Bulgarica
Zdravka Evtimova

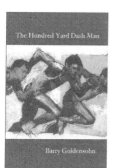

Derail This Train Wreck
Daniel Forbes

Where There Are Two or More
Elizabeth Genovise

The Hundred Yard Dash Man
Barry Goldensohn

Fomite

When You Remember
Deir Yassin
R. L. Green

In A Family Way
Zeke Jarvis

A Free, Unsullied Land
Maggie Kast

Feminist on Fire
Coleen Kearon

Thicker Than Blood
Jan English Leary

A Guide
to the Western
Slope
Roger Lebovitz

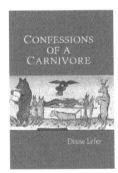

Confessions of a
Carnivore
Diane Lefer

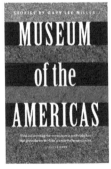

Museum of the
Americas
Gary Lee Miller

My Father's Keeper
Andrew Potok

Fomite

The Hole That Runs
Through Utopia
Joseph D. Reich

Companion Plants
Kathryn Roberts

Rafi's World
Fred Russell

My Murder
and Other Local News
David Schein

Planet Kasper
Volume Two
Peter Schumann

Bread & Sentences
Peter Schumann

Principles of Navigation
Lynn Sloan

Among Angelic Orders
Susan Thoma

Everyone Lives Here
Sharon Webster

Fomite

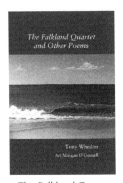

The Falkland Quartet
Tony Whedon

*The Return of
Jason Green*
Suzi Wizowaty

*The Inconveniece
of the Wings*
Silas Dent Zobal

Fomite

More Titles from Fomite...

Fomite

32590727R00126

Made in the USA
Middletown, DE
10 June 2016